Love is
a time of enchantment:
in it all days are fair and all fields
green. Youth is blest by it,
old age made benign: the eyes of love see
roses blooming in December,
and sunshine through rain. Verily
is the time of true-love
a time of enchantment—and
Oh! how eager is woman
to be bewitched!

A DREAM FOR TOMORROW

In her new position as resident nurse at Coombe Magna, Karen Stevens has to bear the enmity of the beautiful Lisa, secretary to the doctor-on-call, Matthew Henshaw. The Hon. Simon Asheby tells Karen that it would be easy to love her, but she knows they can never be more than friends. But the stubborn Dr. Matthew refuses to believe her!

GRACE GOODWIN

A DREAM FOR TOMORROW

Complete and Unabridged

ULVERSCROFT
Leicester

First published in Great Britain in 1987 by
Robert Hale Ltd.,
London

First Large Print Edition
published November 1990
by arrangement with
Robert Hale Ltd.,
London

Copyright © 1987 by Grace Goodwin

British Library CIP Data

Goodwin, Grace
    A dream for tomorrow.—Large print ed.—
Ulverscroft large print series: romance
I. Title
823'.914

ISBN 0-7089-2320-8

Published by
F. A. Thorpe (Publishing) Ltd.
Anstey, Leicestershire
Set by Rowland Phototypesetting Ltd.
Bury St. Edmunds, Suffolk
Printed and bound in Great Britain by
T. J. Press (Padstow) Ltd., Padstow, Cornwall

1

THE apprehension Karen Stevens had been feeling during the long journey there was gradually fading, and she looked with steady eyes across the wide, old leather-topped desk at the thick-set, middle-aged man seated there.

The interview had gone well so far. The hours of duty and the salary offered were good; better than those of dear old St. Catherine's—fondly known as "Kit's". The setting certainly couldn't have been more different either, she mused, from that of Ward 2 West of the big, rambling old teaching hospital in London.

"Well, what do you say, my dear? Think you'd like to join us here?" The man's quizzical faded blue eyes watched her face intently as he rose slowly from the wide chair and came round to her side. "Perhaps you'd like to take a look around, Nurse Stevens, before making up your mind? Of course, it all looks very different during the closed season, but you'll get some idea, I'm sure, of what it'll all look like later on. It's a beautiful spot, and I'm trying hard not to spoil it."

There was a hint of pride in the man's voice, and once more Karen was impressed by what she saw of him. Big, bluff, but with an air of good breeding that his well-worn tweeds could not disguise, he looked more like a typical country squire than the owner of an up-to-date, new holiday complex. And she was very tempted by the proprietor of Coombe Magna's offer. Tall and broad, rather overweight her clinical eye told her, with a high colour to his weather-beaten cheeks that spoke of possible hypertension, he had a good head of grizzled-grey hair, with bushy eyebrows above a pair of well-spaced, kindly eyes. His manner had told her a lot about himself during the interview, and Karen reckoned he was that kind of man who was honest and open, perhaps a little too trusting.

"This is not one of your actual holiday camps, nurse. God forbid! No—not just a country club or holiday complex either. More a mixture of both, if you know what I mean?"

He went back to his desk and the seat groaned a little as he sat down.

"When I had to decide what to do about Coombe Magna—whether to sell or keep it—I had this idea. The alterations to the Manor itself were all done last year before I opened. Then I found I had to expand, take in more guests—so the bungalows are all new this year. Up to now, I've been able to pick and choose my guests— strictly on a 'recommendation only' basis, you understand? No rough element or undesirables if I can possibly help it. And anyone not conforming to rules goes—at once!" He paused and then went on with a smile. "It's an expensive place and we pamper the guests and try to give them good value for their money. So your duties will be rather different from those of a NHS hospital ward I'd say, my dear."

Karen nodded in agreement as he paused, his thick, square-ended fingers pressed together, his eyes holding a far-seeing look in them, the girl opposite him almost forgotten.

"My—my wife had been dead for some time when my only daughter married and went to live in Canada. I missed her so much—it was so lonely. And the upkeep and taxes on Coombe Magna were getting more and more difficult, so . . ." he paused and gave a deep sigh, and then went on, "I had this idea—got a few friends and the bank in on it, and here I am . . ."

He shrugged, his hands splaying wide, his attention coming back to Karen and the interview he was supposed to be conducting in a business-like manner.

"So—how about looking around, nurse? I'll give you a chit and then you can go anywhere you like—before making up your mind finally." He paused again, his blue eyes twinkling. "I hope you do decide to come to us. Good qualifications apart, you'll be an asset, I'm sure."

As he handed Karen the quick-scribbled little note, he smiled at her warmly and she found herself liking this bluff, hearty man. She felt sure he would be easy to work for; a fair-minded employer, and she smiled back at him as she took the note.

"Thanks, Mr. Lyle-Coombe, I'll do that. Look around I mean, and then come back and let you know . . ."

It was probably the greatest decision

she'd had to make in her life as yet. Such different surroundings, different type of patient, quite a change of responsibilities, and leaving behind all her friends at "Kit's " . . .

Once outside, Karen paused, taking in a deep sigh of pure pleasure; it was such a lovely day. Was it an omen, she wondered? One of those early spring days that were so special, so welcome, especially after a winter in London. Even as she looked around her, she fancied she could smell the salty tang of the sea. Slowly turning left, she strolled leisurely along the neat gravelled paths, the discreet bronze sign-plates placed unobtrusively on blocks of granite at the grass verge. The trees and shrubs were all in bud; spring daffodils, tulips and crocus clustered in little patches around the gnarled tree trunks. The close-cropped turf seemed almost newly washed.

As she walked along slowly, Karen came across the many new bungalows, now almost ready for occupation. She was delighted to see how cleverly they blended into their surroundings—nothing brash or cheaply glaring and out of place here, she mused. The thick old trees hid most of the new buildings, and recently planted saplings and bushes helped to conceal the rest. In all sizes—some large enough for a family—others in small quiet terraces suitable for couples, all the bungalows were discreetly grouped, absolute privacy and every comfort assured.

Men were still busy putting the finishing touches; all around her the Coombe Magna resort was getting ready for the coming season. The original old mansion stood proud and firm, as it must have done for centuries. With large, leaded windows, a steep slated roof with tall twisted chimneys, its stonework was charmingly mellowed by the passing years.

Mr. Lyle-Coombe had told her at great length all about the alterations and restorations that had been made inside to adapt it for its new rôle. The vast old cellars were now bright and clean, holding a gymnasium, jacuzzi baths and saunas—all the comforts the right clients were used to. Most of the large bedrooms had their own showers en suite, together with a drinks bar, fridge and television. Modernised as the apartments were, the outside still stood as it had for years, high on the hill, looking down over the beautiful grounds, the lawns and trees, the daffodil dells, the rhododendron banks—and in the near distance, the small cove and the white-laced blue sea.

Proudly the proprietor had pointed out to her the fortunate advantages of that little private bay.

"Can only get at it by the path down there—or the sea, of course. Strictly private, for our guests only . . ." he'd told her.

Slowly Karen made her way through the grounds, admiring the bungalows, the beautifully landscaped gardens. And then, way out of sight, she found the rows of smaller chalets for the seasonal staff, and newly restored sheds now housing shiny red tractors and lawnmowers. Her sensitive nose told her that the old stables held several winter-fat horses, and they snickered and whinnied softly at her approach. Gently rubbing the nose of the nearest, she promised him some lumps of sugar—if she decided to come here, she amended quickly to herself.

She sighed deeply, sorely tempted by what she'd seen up to now, but it was a difficult decision she had to make, wasn't it? Her feet making a soft crunching sound on the gravelled paths, she came to the swimming pool, empty and in the process of being renovated, and with its patio bar tightly shut. Even so, in the pale sunshine, she could well imagine how it would all be later on—could almost hear the excited voices of the holiday makers, of children splashing around at the shallow end; could almost see the lush chaises-longues, the deckchairs, the colourful swimsuits and towels of the sunbathers lying on the broad patios; the discreet service of the swift-footed waiters bringing cool drinks . . .

It was from the far side that she saw then the large balconied dining-room which had been added to the back of the old house. Already the ivy was beginning to spread; the tubs on the balcony ready to bloom, as if the old mansion was drawing this new addition under its benevolent wing. At the moment, the tables and chairs were stacked under dust covers, and the decorators were busy re-painting the high ceiling. Curious, she reached out a hand to push open the heavy swing door leading to the kitchens—"What do *you* want—you can't go in there, miss!"

Startled, Karen turned to see a small, snub-nosed, rather grubby-faced boy watching her warily. His jeans were frayed out at the knees, and already there was a smattering of sun freckles showing across his fairskinned cheeks, and the sunlight shone gleams of gold in the tousled mop of blond hair.

"We're not opened yet," he added, and Karen only just managed to hold back her grin at that important-sounding "we".

"Oh, hello. I've got a paper here that says I can—look around, I mean, anywhere I please. Okay?"

She held out the proprietor's scribbled note solemnly, and just as solemnly the boy reached out a grubby hand and took it, scrutinised it carefully, nodded, and then grudgingly handing it back, replied—

"I suppose so, miss. But don't touch nothing mind, else my Dad'll skin you. He's the head chef here," he finished proudly.

Still restraining her smile and deciding to give the kitchens a miss, Karen managed to look duly impressed and held out her hand.

"I'm Nurse Karen Stevens. What's your name?"

"Ricky. Richard Benjamin Williams."

"How d'you do, Ricky?"

"We live over there." He waved a hand in the direction of a row of cottages at the bottom of the hill, which had been there as long as the big house. "You gonna work here, miss?"

"Er . . ." Karen hesitated. "I don't know yet; I haven't made up my mind yet, Ricky. I might—it's certainly a lovely spot, isn't it?"

"Smashing! Have you seen the baby squirrels—there's lots of 'em. An' I could show you a blackbird's nest," he offered eagerly by way of inducement.

"Well—er—Ricky, unfortunately I've got to catch a train back to London fairly soon, but I tell you what, I'd be glad if you could tell me where I would be working *if* I decided to come here as the nurse in charge, eh?"

Ricky grinned a gap-toothed smile and his skinny chest in its well-washed tee shirt swelled visibly with importance.

"Sure I can. I know all over this place, miss. C'mon, this way!"

So Karen followed him, away from the turquoise-tiled pool and towards the rear entrance to Coombe Magna, to where a neat block slightly set apart was clearly signposted "Medical Unit".

"Aren't you coming in with me then, Ricky?" Karen enquired as the boy seemed to hang back.

"Can't stand the smell, I can't . . ."

"Well, I suppose it smells of paint right now. Look, the painter's kit's still here. Come on, Ricky," she coaxed, and together they entered the bright, anti-septic-smelling building.

Karen was certainly impressed by the cheerful waiting-room with its comfortable chairs, wall pictures, magazine racks and small coffee tables. And certainly no expense had been spared in the extremely well-equipped surgery. Her practised eye told her that everything she was likely to need was at hand; and, thinking of some of the near-derelict units at St. Catherine's, she regarded the Coombe Magna Medical Unit quarters with almost envious approval.

There were two private curtained cubicles—again equipped with everything needed for treatment and examinations; a large, airy sluice, and completely secluded there was a private sick bay consisting of three small rooms, luxuriously furnished for the indisposed guests.

Finally, behind all these, was what was obviously the nurse's own living quarters. A charmingly-furnished living-room, a small bedroom, with a bathroom and kitchen all complete. Standing there looking round, Karen told herself—"I could be happy here. Oh yes, I could enjoy working here . . . and forget . . ."

"Are you coming here then?" Ricky's young voice brought her thoughts back with a jerk. "The other one—the nurse we had last summer—well, she wasn't keen on me."

"Oh, why not, love?" Karen thought the small boy could well turn out to be quite a character. Besides, she had rather a soft spot for tough little boys; she'd handled quite a few in the Children's annexe at "Kit's", hadn't she?

"Said I was a scruffy nuisance, always in here for something, she said. Y'know, cuts and so on . . . So—are you coming here, nurse?" he repeated rather impatiently, and there was a certain appeal in the large round eyes watching hers.

Suddenly, Karen finally made up her mind; not just because Coombe Magna was such a glorious spot; not on Ricky's account, but because the post would be something so different, a challenge, a change and a chance to get away from St. Catherine's and all the bitter memories . . .

"Yes, Ricky, old son," she answered slowly, "I think I'll be coming here, and I'll keep you to your promise to show me all the things in the grounds when I do come. Okay?"

Ricky's eyes gleamed, his snub nose wrinkling with delight.

"Okay, nurse, you're on!"

And solemnly Karen shook his grubby hand and felt she'd made one friend here already.

"Thanks, Ricky. Be seeing you then—next month," and with one last satisfied look round the cosy living-room, she closed the doors of the Medical Unit firmly and went to give her new employer her decision.

John Lyle-Coombe seemed equally delighted at her news a little later.

"I'll give in my notice at once then," Karen told him as they finished their chat.

Karen caught her train with only a few minutes to spare, and with a faint sigh of relief she took a corner seat. Relieved, too, that she had made up her mind and got the new post, for as far as she could tell, it would be a pleasant one. She liked the look of the Medical Unit and her own quarters; she had certainly taken to its owner, John Lyle-Coombe . . . and Ricky!

As she turned to watch the houses and the lines of washing, the handkerchief-sized lawns and back gardens, all exposed to the view of passing trains, she also saw her own reflection in the grimy carriage window. Saw her smooth, short, chestnut-brown hair, layered neatly to her head and so suitable for the little white cap usually perched upon it; saw the wide, brown eyes that, had she known it, often gave away her innermost feelings. She was convinced that her mouth was too generous, that her nose was almost retroussé. Just then her face was in repose, but her chin could stick out defiantly when Nurse Karen Stevens was on the warpath!

She stirred restlessly in her seat. Not the sort of face to launch a thousand ships! But then, she grinned wryly, who wanted to launch a thousand ships these days? She often longed to be a shade taller, for she had the idea that a little more height would make her, well—look more important somehow. And certainly all the different belts clinching the various coloured dresses she'd worn from being a student nurse to senior SRN at "Kit's" had never helped to disguise her well-rounded figure, she mused ruefully.

That her features were a mixture of Madonna and minx; that she was small and cuddly and altogether lovable, never occurred to Karen. She had always been far too busy to be vain about her looks. Besides, she thought as she sat there with the fields and roads and houses flying by, her looks hadn't been good enough to keep Keith, had they?

And for once she was alone, with time to spare, with nothing else to keep the memories and heartache at bay, and she gave herself up—indulging herself as she rarely did—to remembering her lost love . . .

She had been in her second year at St. Catherine's when she and Keith had become a pair. She had been very young, still delighted by the thrill of living and working in London, away from the rather sheltered life of her father's little country practice, and her mother's round of good works in the village. She had left home wide-eyed, excitedly looking forward to making new friends, passing her exams and fulfilling her earliest ambitions—to be a good nurse and to get away from the restrictions of being an only child.

She was lucky to be one of the fortunate nurses allowed to share a flat away from the Nurses' Home attached to the hospital; away from the eagle eye of sister-in-charge there. From the very start, the flat had been somewhere for the hungry students, medical and nursing alike, to drop in. They had a lot in common—they all worked at "Kit's", were always broke and needed to make new friends. As long as the strict curfew was adhered to, no one complained, for the whole of the huge, old house was sub-let to nurses. There was always a great deal of clatter and chatter; much borrowing and lending; sharing of disasters and news, good or bad. That is until the time for exams loomed in the offing, and then silence descended like a pall; young faces took on a strained anxious look; frantic questions and answers were tossed back and forth, note-books well thumbed!

Karen and her room-mate, Sue, were helping the latest batch of young doctors to celebrate, or commiserate, their exam results when she met Keith Thomas. Really met him socially, that is, without his white coat and stethoscope as one of a group usually trailing behind a consultant.

"That dress looks good on you, Karen. You look different somehow out of uniform, I mean."

And she had glanced up quickly to look into the light blue eyes of Dr. Keith Thomas. His tall, slim figure towered above hers; his fair hair catching the light from the solitary lamp, making a halo of gold around his well-shaped head. His clothes, casual as were all those there, were expensively cut, and the fragrance of some exclusive aftershave had banished the usual antiseptic smell of the hospital. Not a very original line, but Karen's heart had started to beat faster at the open admiration in Keith's eyes. The firm touch of his hand on her arm made her nerves tingle as he led her away from the crowd around them.

"It's time you and I got to know each other, young Karen." His voice was warm and invitingly gentle. "Now then . . ."

And they spent the rest of that party sitting on the stairs, chatting together, oblivious of passing feet and legs, finding so much to discover about each other.

Right from the start, Karen knew how ambitious Keith was; he was clever and keen to get on as quickly as he could, to specialise and be able to set up in a good practice. Still, Karen was keen, too, to become a staff nurse and then a sister, and falling in love wasn't on the cards, not right then! But as she and Keith spent more and more of their free time together, they were soon paired off by that ever-knowing grapevine of hospital gossip.

Karen and Keith—even their very names went together . . .

Keith's lovemaking became increasingly demanding and passionate, and Karen found it hard at times not to lose herself to him totally.

"It's no use, Keith, it'll be ages and ages before we're able to marry. Let's not get too involved—in too deep . . ."

And only she knew how difficult it was to keep Keith at arm's length, for his sake as well as her own. He was her first love and she gave him her young heart wholly, longing to belong to him completely, but some instinct made her hold back—to wait a while . . .

Her eyes still unseeing as the train rattled on, she looked back, realising that *she* had been the one to mention marriage, not Keith. Oh, he had said he loved her and wanted her many times, but had never spoken of their future together—not in so many words. And the thought brought a wry twist to the usually tender mouth of the girl seated there.

Karen had passed her finals without undue difficulty, to emerge a fully-fledged SRN. She was given more and more responsibility, learning all the time, often standing in for ward sister on several different wards; enjoying her work, happy in her love for the good-looking doctor. She was competent, cool and kind, not given to moods or sloppy work, and was liked by patients and respected by the staff. If at times she wondered why Keith didn't discuss their future, well—he was busy and ambitious and could probably be waiting to offer her a more secure one. And theirs was a comfortable, happy relationship and she wanted no other man in her life.

The winter had set in early and was at its worst just before Christmas, with scarcely a bed to spare in the hospital. Nurses and doctors were run off their feet, the hours long with little time for proper meals or sleep, and Karen went down with a bad dose of 'flu. And for the first time in her young life felt wretchedly ill.

She was to go home on sick leave, and saying goodbye to Keith made it all the more miserable, too.

"I'll miss you, darling. What a rotten Christmas here without you." As Keith made to take her in his arms, Karen croaked—

"Don't, love. I'm crawling with 'flu bugs, I'm sure." That she looked dreadful didn't help either. "Can't you come down to us for Christmas? My folks would love to have you—please, Keith, do."

Weakness made the silly tears prickle behind her brown eyes; she felt so low and miserable. Keith shook his head, his eyes not quite meeting hers as he murmured—

"I can't, Karen my darling. I promised my folks I'd go home this year. They're inviting a houseful of friends expecting to see me. But I'll phone you every day. I'll miss you like hell, sweetheart, and we'll celebrate the New Year together, I promise . . ."

Seated there in the dusty railway carriage, remembering it all so clearly, Karen couldn't help her lips curling in bitterness.

"I promise . . ." Keith had said. The days had passed agonisingly slowly in spite of the fuss and loving care of her parents, with only one phone call from Keith asking if she'd arrived home safely, and once more bemoaning the fact that they wouldn't be together for Christmas.

Finding it hard to take an interest in her mother's busy preparations, desultorily answering her GP father's questions about life at St. Catherine's, she had finally decided on Christmas Eve to call Keith's home. With the hall door closed, she had waited, clutching the receiver with trembling hands, her knees suddenly weak. There were sounds of a party in the background coming over the wires, and someone was "finding old Keith" for her as she hung on.

She told herself that the 'flu had left her low and depressed, but she was sure she had felt the difference in Keith's manner even over the telephone.

Yes, he was fine, he answered, how was she? Feeling better? Oh, good! It might have been any casual acquaintance on the other end of the line, and Karen's throat had tightened with dismay and foreboding. Keith seemed in a hurry to hang up and get back to his party, and with a half-hearted—

"See you soon, Karen," had done so, leaving her numb with unhappiness. No loving message, no mention of missing her, nothing . . .

And back to the warmth of the log fire in the lounge, her mother had tut-tutted at the sight of her daughter's wan face and had insisted upon keeping her at home on sick leave for a week longer, in spite of Karen's anxiety to get back to St. Catherine's, to Keith and her ward.

She was still feeling a bit shaky as she unpacked, and for once she wished her room-mate would stop fussing around and treating her like one of her own patients.

"For heaven's sake, Sue, cut out the Flo Nightingale bit, love, it's 'flu I've had, nothing worse . . ."

But Sue had stood there, unconsciously pleating and re-pleating the hem of one of Karen's garments between her fingers, her usual sunny, open face miserable and anxious-looking. Until Karen, looking up into her friend's eyes, asked—

"What's wrong, Sue? You look a bit upset, love."

The other girl had swallowed visibly and then began with a rush—

"I'd better tell you, Karen before— before you hear it from someone else . . ." she paused, obviously reluctant to go on.

"Tell me what?" Karen felt a chill pass over her then; it wasn't like Sue to act like this, was it?

"It's Keith," Sue blurted out angrily. "He's—oh, I could kill him! He's got himself engaged!"

Shock had hit Karen then like a real physical blow.

"Engaged?" she gasped unbelieving.

"Yes, that's right. Over Christmas it was—to the daughter of a Harley Street man—a big noise, a specialist and filthy rich to boot. A friend of Keith's family it seems. And she's his only child. Oh, he's done very well for himself has our Keith." Sue's voice had been full of suppressed anger and bitterness on Karen's behalf.

It was the sympathy and pitying glances of her colleagues that Karen found hardest to bear. She was still stunned at the news of Keith's defection; still feeling low after the 'flu, and she couldn't bear the overt glances, the whispering that followed her as she went about her work.

She avoided the staff canteen as assiduously as Keith was avoiding her, for apart from a brief wave of the hand in greeting as he sped, white coat flying open, down the corridor past her ward, she hadn't heard from him at all.

Then after a week of hiding herself away, of indulging in heartache and tears, Karen's natural sturdy spirit began to assert itself. Why should she mourn the loss of a man who so obviously hadn't loved her? She could hardly say she'd been jilted, could she—they hadn't been engaged, no plans made.

Her stubborn chin had squared itself, and with a shade more make-up as a disguise, she sallied forth—to start to live without Keith. She even forced herself to send a little note round to his rooms.

"Congratulations, Keith. I hear you're about to make a wonderful marriage for yourself. I would have preferred to hear the news from your own lips, still—no hard feelings! Good luck—Karen."

She was proud of the effort, telling herself that it was his new fiancée who would need all the luck, and that Keith, with his overpowering ambition, was no great loss, was he?

All the same, working at St. Catherine's

suddenly lost all its appeal, and after much heart-searching, Karen decided to make a move, to have a complete change. Before she could lose her courage, she placed her name with the Nursing Agency requesting the chance of a free-lance or private nursing position. To her surprise, a request to call in to hear about something they had to offer came in a very short time.

And sitting upright in the hard chair, Karen couldn't help but voice her surprise when the post was described to her.

"A holiday camp?" She couldn't keep the doubt out of her voice.

"Oh, dear me, no! Not quite. Definitely a little more, er—select than that!"

The principal pushed her spectacles further up her bony nose and shuffled the papers on the desk before her.

"It's a fine old mansion in a lovely spot on the coast, Nurse Stevens. In beautiful grounds, I'm told, quite an, er—expensive holiday place, and you would be in charge of the Medical Unit and First Aid Post. There's a nearby doctor on call for anything serious; he comes in twice a week to hold a surgery session. There is an excellent private bed wing in the local hospital. All found—and your own quarters, too."

She paused and looked across her desk at Karen's rather wan-looking face.

"Do you good, my dear, all that sea air and good food in such pleasant surroundings," she said kindly. And then more briskly she went on—"Anyway, Mr. Lyle-Coombe, the owner, will see you next Wednesday, fares and expenses paid. Shall I tell him you'll go for an interview, Nurse Stevens?"

It certainly sounded far enough away from St. Catherine's and utterly different, Karen mused. So she nodded.

"Yes, please," she answered, and collecting all the details and instructions on how to reach Coombe Magna Hall, she thanked the older woman for her trouble, took the proffered note of introduction and left. She had made her first decisive step towards forgetting Keith . . .

As soon as she got back to London after her trip to Coombe Magna, Karen lost no time in asking to see the Chief Nursing Officer. After telling her all about the new post, she gave in her month's notice, her soft lips struggling to stop their trembling. And the woman seated on the other side of the wide desk, all-seeing, all-wise, accepted this with good grace.

"I'll be sorry to lose you, of course, Nurse Stevens. You've always been one of my most reliable nurses, so I wish you luck in this new post. I'll forward your papers and so on to the Agency. And please—let me know if there is any way I can help you. Good luck, Karen my dear, and don't forget all you've learned here, will you?"

Karen shook her head and swallowed hard, her throat tight. "I won't . . ."

In spite of her protests, Sue and a few of their set insisted on giving Karen a farewell party.

"We'll all miss you, love. At least let us give you a good send-off." As usual no formal invitations were issued—everyone just turned up if and when they were off-duty, and the small flat was bursting at the seams with nurses and young doctors in training. White coats, belts and caps were cast aside, and practically everybody was in stockinged feet, and the noise was deafening.

Everyone was curious and wanted to know about her new post, tactfully refraining from mentioning Keith's name, but Karen knew there were quite a few who were longing to do so! Things were really hotting up when, halfway through the evening, there was a sudden unexpected hush and Karen looked up—to see Keith's tall slim figure in the doorway, and her heart jerked and then went on thudding painfully, her face pale and tense.

For a few seconds, she was speechless, and then pride came to her aid and her chin squared defiantly; she was determined not to let him know how deeply his engagement to another girl had hurt her. The smile almost cracked her face as she called out brightly—

"Hi, Keith, glad you could make it. Can I get you a drink?" It was an effort, but Karen was proud of the steadiness of her voice and her lips twisted wryly as she saw the obvious relief on Keith's face. Had he expected her to make a scene; was his appearance here tonight just his way of facing her again—in public? Where she couldn't make a scene anyway?

"Er—thanks, Karen. Thought I'd just drop in and—and wish you all the best for the new job."

Her steady brown eyes looked at him for a moment, noticing the dull flush on his cheeks.

"Of course, Keith. Come in and join the gang . . ." and he accepted the glass of punch with an assumed casual air.

"Thought you were a fixture at 'Kit's ', Karen?"

Again pride came to her rescue and made her tell the white lie.

"Oh, this has been arranged for quite a while, Keith, didn't you know?" And she turned to have her glass refilled, hoping no one saw her shaking hand.

Keith didn't stay long, and as if to cover up his departure, Karen's friends threw themselves noisily into making the party even more of a success. And after he'd left, some of the strain left her face as she strove to enjoy herself. She would miss these friends, she knew.

And her last day came round all too swiftly, with quite a wrench for Karen, for after all, she had spent all her nursing days between the walls of St. Catherine's.

"Good lord, Karen my girl," she told herself firmly, "twenty-four's too young to get into a rut anyway."

All the same, her tears of farewell matched Sue's.

"Keep in touch, won't you, Karen love? Promise?"

"I promise, Sue . . ."

So Karen packed all her cherished bits and pieces, together with the new white uniform dresses and caps she'd bought for her new post, and went home until it was time to travel to Coombe Magna.

Spring was well advanced when Karen's taxi deposited her and her luggage outside the reception office at Coombe Magna. The leaves on the trees were almost fully grown in every shade of green; the flower beds were bright with spring flowers, the bungalows ready for their first visitors. The maids were busy, chatting and laughing, hurrying to and fro with arms and trolleys laden with clean, fresh linen. Lawns were getting their final trim, the pool was ready for the first hardy swimmers, and there was a clatter of pots and pans from the kitchens where the cooks were already starting the meals for the staff. All around her, Karen felt the buzz of excitement and anticipation—everything looked so bright and comfortable—expensively so.

The girl in the reception office was smart and intelligent-looking and her shelves were well-stocked with colourful brochures, apartment keys all hanging ready on the empty pigeonholes.

"I'll tell Mr. John you're here, nurse." The young receptionist picked up the telephone as she smiled her welcome.

John Lyle-Coombe's greeting was warm and hearty, bringing a responsive smile to Karen's face, making her feel at home at once.

"Ah, good to see you, nurse. Good journey? Here's your keys; check them over and be sure to let me know if there's anything else you need across there . . ." he waved his large hand in the direction of the Medical Unit. "I think you'll find everything ready for you. Remember, it's your own little domain, nurse. Mrs. Roberts will relieve you; see her and arrange things between you; though—you're in charge—remember that."

Again his ruddy face beamed down at her.

"Hope you settle in all right, my dear. We open in two days—think you can be ready?"

Karen took the bunch of keys and nodded.

"Thank you, Mr. John—I'm sure I shall be," she answered quietly, liking this big, bluff man more than ever. Mr. John to his guests and employees alike, she found later.

"Good! There's a list of the doctor's surgery times, too. It's not too far away—I'll leave you to contact him, shall I? Now let me see . . ." he pulled his ear, a habit Karen was to notice many times in the future. "You'll have your own regular cleaner—takes her instructions from you. You can eat in the staff dining-room or not, nurse, please yourself. Things will be quiet at first, but once the season gets well under way, you'll be busy enough, I can tell you!"

Just then the phone rang and he was called back to his own office in the big house, and with an assuring smile for Karen, he hurried away.

"I've sent a porter across with your bags, nurse," the receptionist's voice was friendly, and with a murmur of thanks, Karen went outside.

The air was fresh and clear; everything around her clean and bright, ready to begin a new season. A new beginning for Karen too . . .

The Medical Unit still smelled of paint, and she threw open the windows immediately, looking around with a professional, assessing eye, making mental notes of several small alterations she would be making. Going through to her own quarters, she gave a deep sigh of pleasure as she started to unpack, thinking of ways she could begin making her domain more homely and personal.

Half way through, she stopped to make herself a cup of tea, and as if on cue, a tousled head appeared round the kitchen door. With a start, Karen looked up to see Ricky's snub-nosed, freckled face beaming at her.

"Hi, nurse! You did come then. Gee—that's great!"

"Hello, Ricky. Nice to see you again."
She paused, unfolding the garment in her
hands slowly. Then she went on firmly,
"One thing though, love, please knock if
you want to come in here to see me in my
quarters, eh? And no popping in during
surgery hours either."

The smile faded from the young face at
her words, so she added warmly—

"Otherwise, I'm glad to see you, Ricky.
After all, you're my first friend here, you
know," and she saw his grin return.

"Well, I've brought you something,
nurse. Sort of present, like," and with a
glint of mischief in his eyes she failed to
notice, he stretched out a grubby paw.

Automatically, gratefully, Karen held
out her hand, but as Ricky placed that
something on her outstretched palm, she
almost shrieked aloud. Just in time she
steeled herself not to recoil or drop it, for
in that same moment, she saw Ricky's eyes
watching her face intently and she knew
he was testing her out! For there on her
hand, its soft pink nose twitching, its little
bright red eyes wary, was a small white
mouse!

Karen had her fair share of courage, but

like most females, she recoiled at the sight of a mouse!

"Oh, it's—er—lovely, Ricky," and she couldn't quite keep the tremor out of her voice.

"It's quite tame, miss. And nice an' clean. I've had him a long time . . ."

"Well, I think that's very good of you, love, to want me to have him, but I wonder—could you still look after him for me? I'm going to be pretty busy around here, and I'll need all the help I can get."

She watched the skinny chest grow inches bigger. "'Course I will," he replied stoutly. "C'mon, you," and he pushed the white mouse back into his pocket.

"Wash your hands, Ricky, and you can have some tea with me, eh?"

She opened the tin of fancy biscuits so thoughtfully provided by Coombe Magna —and made a friend for life. From now on Ricky was her man . . .

2

THE next morning she threw open all the windows again, and then, with a plastic apron over her white dress, her cap perched perilously on top of her smooth, chestnut-coloured hair, she set to putting things to order—her idea of order.

She scrubbed out all the cupboards, and as she did so, memory took her back to her early student days. Then, before she should start remembering Keith, she took up the "dangerous" list and began meticulously checking it off against the drugs in the cupboard that was always kept locked. Assured that all was correct, she started a new case book, noted down one or two further requisitions, and generally enjoyed herself!

It felt good to be completely in charge; to arrange everything in her own way, and if she wondered whether she would always think so; whether she would always be able to cope, she dismissed the little niggle and made herself a mug of coffee, surveying her little kingdom with a feeling of satisfaction.

She had several minor casualties amongst the staff that first day—a deep cut and a slight burn from the kitchens, a gardener with a septic wound from a thorn buried deep in his finger. She had a tough time convincing the solid old countryman that an anti-tetanus injection was necessary, but firmness and a little persuasion won the day.

Staff mealtimes were to be later than those of the guests, and that first evening was to be no exception it seemed, and Karen, her day's work finished, decided she would have time for a quick look around the little fishing port. It was only a few minutes' walk to one of the main roads leading into the centre.

Then she had a sudden inspiration, and she consulted one of the lists Mr. John had given her. Yes, she would go and make herself known to the doctor with whom she was to work for the rest of the summer. She reckoned that by the time she got there, he would be finished his evening surgery.

It was a typical coastal town that had

sprawled out, growing from a tiny fishing harbour into a busy seaside town. Now it was just opening up for the new season, re-stocking and stirring after its long winter slumber. The gift shops looked freshly painted and inviting, and in between were lovely old black and white timbered houses turned into teashops and restaurants, opposite open-fronted stalls selling freshly caught lobsters, crabs and other shellfish. Cobbled streets sloped up and away from the main shopping centre, and it was in the corner of one of these that Karen found the doctor's premises.

It was a tall, narrow three-storeyed building with shining brass nameplates and the usual surgery lamp over a side door. Climbing the worn old steps, Karen walked into a typical doctor's waiting-room, with chairs round three of its walls, and a table of glossy magazines in the centre. The secretary's file-lined cubicle was behind a frosted-glass partition, with doors to the doctors' consulting rooms on either side.

Gazing around with interest, Karen was brought sharply down to earth by the brisk voice addressing her—

"Have you an appointment?"

The girl facing her was tall and slim, much taller than Karen herself. Her blue-black hair was held loosely in the nape of her slender neck, and her skin was thick-cream smooth. But it was the cold unfriendliness in the girl's dark blue eyes that chilled and startled Karen.

"Er—no," she stammered, and then conscious of the interested, listening patients still seated there waiting to see a doctor, she went on more steadily—"No, I haven't an appointment, but I'll wait until Dr. Henshaw has finished seeing all his patients, if I may? Would you please let him know that I'm waiting, though? I'm Nurse Stevens and I'm taking over duty at the Medical Unit at Coombe Magna."

Whilst she was talking, the other girl's eyes had been looking her over with cool deliberation and with no trace of warmth in them, and Karen began to feel annoyed. Just who did this girl think she was? Looking down at the nameplate on the front edge of the desk, she saw the words—

"Lisa Felstead—secretary."

"Well, Lisa Felstead, I'm glad I'm not a patient coming here," Karen thought to herself.

"I'll tell Doctor. Please take a seat," she was told offhandedly.

As she sat there glancing through a glossy magazine, Karen could feel the interested eyes of the few remaining patients on her, and automatically she began diagnosing to herself each of their complaints—the little old lady, twisted and gnarled with arthritis; the big, florid-faced man who was possibly pickling his liver with too many tots of liquor. Here a high blood pressure, there an anaemic, then the obviously pregnant. One saw them all at some time or another in hospital.

As the last patient left, Karen put aside the magazine, preparing to go in to meet the doctor, but after a further long wait, the secretary still hadn't called her name, so Karen rose to tap on the glass partition. It was so quiet by then that she had a feeling that she was the only person left there. There was no reply to her knock and Karen bit her lip; what should she do now? Had Dr. Henshaw been called away on an emergency? But there was no sound coming from behind the partition or either of the doctors' rooms.

Karen's temper started to rise; this was certainly a churlish way to treat anyone, especially one of the profession—just to leave her sitting there! Then to her relief a door opened and a man came out quickly, obviously not expecting to see anyone else in the waiting-room. Her temper still simmering, Karen waited, her tawny eyes chill.

He was over average height, squarely built with shoulders of an athlete rather than a doctor. His weather-tanned face was one of typical ruggedness; an ordinary, pleasant-looking face, with a mop of unruly brown hair in need of a trim. Level dark brown eyes, a strong chin below a nose that had a bump on its ridge, probably, she mused, from some old rugger injury—there was something solid and dependable-looking about him, Karen thought swiftly. Surely not the type to leave a nurse—a new colleague-to-be—ignored?

His dark eyes widened at the sight of her, and Karen couldn't help noticing the thick eyelashes—so wasted on a man—and the beginning of a charming lop-sided smile.

"I'm sorry, I thought everyone had gone —thought I was through evening surgery. Can I help you?"

Karen's lips tightened. So Lisa Felstead hadn't given the doctor her message, or had he forgotten?

"Are you going out on an emergency, doctor?" Karen's voice was professionally cool, and Dr. Henshaw's thick eyebrows rose in query.

"No, I've finished—or thought I was . . ."

"Oh! In that case, can you spare me a few minutes, doctor? I'm Nurse Karen Stevens, and I've just taken up the appointment as SRN at Coombe Magna's medical unit. I understand you are the visiting doctor there? So I thought I would just come in and make myself known to you . . ."

Karen's voice sounded aloof and unfriendly as she gave her explanation, but she was still rather cross at being left hanging about there. Again those eyebrows made a question mark.

"Then for heaven's sake, girl, why didn't you send your name in? It's a wonder I didn't leave by the other door into my living quarters."

There was a touch of annoyance in his voice then—probably needing his evening meal just then!

"I explained who I was to your secretary, doctor, and asked if she would ask you to see me. I thought we might save time if I used this free evening to come and make your acquaintance," she repeated.

"You told Lisa—Miss Felstead. . . ?" His voice sounded incredulous and Karen's face flushed. Did he think she was lying? "My secretary never forgets messages," Dr. Henshaw finished hardily.

"Well, this time she did!" Karen replied emphatically. Her heart sank and she swallowed hard; this certainly wasn't a very good start, was it? Her sole idea of coming here tonight had been to get to know Dr. Henshaw—to start off right. And something in that face of his told her he didn't suffer fools gladly!

Karen had a feeling that somehow Lisa Felstead had deliberately refrained from letting her employer know he had a visitor waiting. But why? They had never met before; was she always so coldly off-hand and neglectful? Not the best of qualities for a surgery receptionist, surely? Still Lisa Felstead was beautiful to look at, and perhaps this young doctor and his partner preferred haughty brunettes?

"Well, Nurse—er—Stevens, I'm just about to stretch my legs a little while before dinner. Come on, we'll take the cliff road from behind here," he indicated rear-wards with a nod of his head, "and I'll walk with you part of my way back to Coombe Magna. Okay?"

Without waiting for her reply, he opened the door and strode out ahead, to be joined outside by a fat old corgi with alertly pricked ears and large, liquid-brown eyes that gazed up at him adoringly —with no tail to wag, he was shaking the whole of his solid rump in welcoming ecstasy.

Karen found she had to stride out to keep up with him, and was thankful that he had to pause occasionally to allow the dog's short legs to catch up at least. During one such pause, he pointed out—

"It's quiet just now—for the practice, I mean. Hotel keepers, landladies and so on are apt to forget what ails them once the busy season gets under way. This'll soon be crowded," and as he indicated the empty rugged path that wound round the cliff top, Karen wondered if he resented the holiday-makers or not?

As they waited for the corgi to catch up, she looked round, finding the view from up there breathtakingly wonderful. There were two small bays below, probably others further round out of sight, but from where they stood the headlands jutting out completely enclosed the bays, making them entirely secluded and safe.

"That's Hightower Head," the doctor pointed to the slender white lighthouse topping the headland to their right, "and the smaller bay is Asheby Bay—for the exclusive use of Coombe Magna visitors only!"

Indeed, Karen could just glimpse the tall chimneys of Coombe Magna Hall from where they stood, but at that moment, she was wondering just what had put that bitter note in her companion's voice.

"Asheby Bay?" Karen repeated and Dr.

Henshaw turned to face her, a dark frown creasing his broad forehead, and with a slight twist to his lips, he answered—

"Yes, sold to Mr. John Lyle-Coombe for a nice fat sum, I don't doubt, by the heir's to Asheby Manor!"

This time there could be no mistaking the bitterness in his words, the reason for that frown.

"Asheby Manor, back behind there, home of the Ashebys for centuries, now in the hands of the Hon. Simon—damn him!"

"What—for selling that bay to Coombe Magna? It's one of the resort's best features—a private beach, safe, accessible and secluded."

"I might as well tell you, nurse; you'll hear it soon enough anyway. I've been fighting ever since I came here to get Simon Asheby to sell the council a plot of land to build a new Maternity Centre on. A piece away from the tourist trade, yet easily reached, with good access and near to the 'bus routes and so on. Oh yes," he went on flatly, "he's got a piece just right for it, but he won't sell!"

"Why ever not?" Karen put in.

"Because the council can't offer the sort of money the Hon. Simon obviously got from your Mr. John Lyle-Coombe, that's why," Dr. Henshaw finished angrily, and he kicked out savagely, scuffing the loose shale of the path beneath their feet. "Old boys together, those two, I reckon."

Karen decided she didn't much like the sound of Simon Asheby, but she had met the owner of the Coombe Magna complex, and he certainly hadn't struck her as being a heartless type of man. And this young Dr. Henshaw seemed to have a large-sized chip on his shoulder about landowners, with one man in particular.

But local politics wouldn't be her concern, but the guests of Coombe Magna would be, so, with a slight shrug, she deftly turned the conversation round to the leisure resort and what she was likely to come up against there.

"There was quite a bit of local opposition to this holiday resort venture," Dr. Henshaw added when they had discussed several aspects of her job there.

"Local opposition—why?" Karen turned to look at him in surprise and saw a lopsided smile round his firm mouth.

"Well, look at it this way, nurse. Coombe Magna takes guests the local hotels could do with. They spend their money inside the complex and very little in the town itself. John Lyle-Coombe grows most of his own stuff—buys the rest wholesale naturally." He spread his square-tipped fingers wide. "It's too self-contained and the profits from it are all channelled one way—into his own pocket."

"And yet you . . ." Karen began impulsively, and then bit her tongue. It wasn't her place to question why, if he was so much against all her new employer had accomplished, he, Dr. Matthew Henshaw, was willing to attend the guests there and do two surgeries a week.

But the tall man watching her face in the gathering dusk read her thoughts clearly, and his eyes darkened.

"Why I work for Coombe Magna? Wasn't that what you were about to ask? Well, Nurse Stevens, because I'm new here, too, and new doctors with new ideas have to prove themselves to the wary folks around here."

There was a harsh raggedness in his

voice that betrayed some deep resentment, something that bothered him greatly. He stopped and held out his hand.

"This is as far as I'm going. Good evening, nurse . . ."

He whistled to the dog, spun on his heels and turned back the way they had come, leaving a somewhat disconcerted Karen gazing at his retreating back.

Karen passed over the small key to Mrs. Roberts, the St. John's nurse who was to take over in her off-duty times. Rather plump and sturdy, she was a pleasant, homely-looking North Country woman, and seemed to be the unflappable, capable type of nurse that Karen liked to work with. Getting to know her over a cup of tea and a long chat, she reckoned she could trust Mrs. Roberts not to let her down.

"I'll always leave you a note saying just where I can be found, Mrs. Roberts, in that little drawer there," Karen indicated, "along with the case book and any other details you should have. If you do the same, we'll always be able to keep in contact. Is that all right with you?"

"That's fine, Nurse Stevens. I'll have the key with me and do the same."

Karen gave a sigh of satisfaction.

"That's settled then. And please—call me Karen when we're alone together like this, Mrs. Roberts." She smiled across at the older woman, who gave her an answering smile, and both knew that a good working relationship had been established that morning.

"Now about times off . . ." Karen added, and went on to spend a little while working these out, although Mrs. Roberts insisted that they could be fairly fluid; she only had her husband, a local fisherman, to look after, and as she put it "he can fend for himself quite well, if needs be, er —Karen."

"I'll always be in myself for Dr. Henshaw's surgeries, of course," Karen told her and would have liked to ask Mrs. Roberts how she got on with the doctor, but then decided it would be rather unethical to discuss him behind his back.

However, at the mention of his name, Mrs. Roberts' face sobered a little.

"That would be best, I've not had a lot to do with him yet. I prefer one of the older doctors myself. Dr. Henshaw's young—full of new-fangled ideas, but he'll learn, given time. We don't go in for fancy changes much round here, nurse—er—Karen," she finished.

"But surely the new Maternity Centre would be a good thing, Mrs. Roberts, beneficial to everyone?"

Mrs. Roberts sniffed audibly.

"I dare say, but it'll take a lot of hard work to convince the townsfolk of that!" she said flatly. "We've got along with the old one well enough."

Just then there was the sound of the outer door opening and a clear voice calling—

"Anyone at home?" and Mrs. Roberts rose to go as a young woman breezed through as if she knew her way around. She paused in the doorway and Karen looked up to see Penny Naylor, the resort's chief entertainment hostess. Along with her husband, Pete, she was responsible for organising the entertainments put on to keep the guests, young and old, happy. Karen had seen her around, but as yet had to meet her close to. She was really lovely, with her clear skin and bright, laughing eyes; her fair hair shone and she looked brimming with health and energy.

"I'll go then, nurse." Mrs. Roberts excused herself, leaving the two girls alone.

After introducing herself, Penny asked—

"Can you help me, Karen, look. . . ?" and she held up her slender foot for inspection; she had an angry-looking blister on her heel.

"M'mm, nasty. I'll have to prick it, Penny, I'm afraid. How on earth did you manage to get that?"

"Vanity, nurse, sheer vanity," Penny laughed showing her lovely white teeth. "Went dancing in some gorgeous new shoes, and they were killing me all night!"

Karen pressed a sterile pad to the deflated blister and then carefully applied a dressing.

"Keep this on, Penny, and don't wear those shoes—well, not for a while anyway," she grinned. Hadn't she herself, like all females, suffered in the cause of vanity?

"Oh thanks, that feels much better. You've got a nice touch, Karen. Do you ever get sore feet? Mine take a terrible pounding in the high season."

"I certainly did in my student days. We all used to bathe our feet, dry them well and then rub in surgical spirit to make the skin tougher. Plenty of talc and that was it; you should try it, Penny," Karen suggested.

"Will do—thanks," and while Karen made two mugs of coffee, Penny began to tell her what her job entailed.

"The boss is a bit of a stick-in-the-mud really. Won't let us have a pop group in. In fact, no music at all after midnight! Bit tough on the teenagers, I reckon," Penny went on, and from her chatter, Karen gathered that she and Pete would dearly love to "liven the place up a bit".

Secretly, Karen rather agreed with Mr. John's desire to reserve Coombe Magna as it was, exclusive and unspoilt, keeping out the more rowdy element. There were plenty of large holiday camp type resorts for those who wanted that type of vacation. Still, from what Penny told her that morning, she and Pete had plenty of good ideas for giving guests a choice of things to do. There was scuba diving, underwater snorkelling, water ski-ing, water polo, as well as a nearby golf course, and the Hall had its own saunas and stables—the choice was endless when money was no object!

"We put up lists in the games rooms and those who want to join in any competitions put their names and table numbers on the list. They make up their own teams, partners, foursomes, and so on, and the heats winners then contact the next on the list. No urging by Pete or me, no cajoling—all easy and carefree. The boss insists upon it! Folks join in or not, of their own accord. We just see that the lists are changed; supervise the finals; referee matches and hand out the prizes and lots of chat at the end of each week." Penny paused for breath, her bright eyes dancing. "By the way, whenever you're going out shopping, please bring in some for us. We're always running short of presents, and things like chalk, various oddments like that."

"I certainly will," Karen promised. She liked this cheerful, pretty girl. Here, at least, was one healthy member of the staff;

she was brimming over with energy and vigour.

"By the way, Penny," she asked later. "Am I allowed to use the sports facilities —pool, tennis courts?"

"Well, last year's nurse did," Penny told her, "but we're more fully booked this year than last—only just opened then —so I'd check with the boss if I were you."

So at the first opportunity, Karen went along to Mr. John's office to ask him, and to her delight, he not only agreed, but asked her—

"Do you ride at all, nurse?"

"Well, I used to a bit before I started nursing," Karen looked at him eagerly. "Oh, I'd love to. Could I really use one of your horses?"

"You surely can, my dear. Tell the head stable boy I said you could. And there's one of my daughter's hard hats I'll look out for you, if you like?"

"Thanks. Oh, thank you very much." Karen's beaming smile got a friendly nod in return from her boss.

And that was how Karen came to be out riding a few days later. It was a lovely morning; the dawn's sea mist had dispersed early with the appearance of the sun, and she set out, gingerly at first, then gaining more confidence as she went along. The mare, Brown Belle, was a placid, velvet-mouthed creature, inclined to make her own pace, but she seemed to be quite happy with her new rider.

The bridle path wound up and away from Coombe Magna and the sea; skirted the fields and hedges, almost non-existent at times, well-trodden at others. Gaining courage, Karen urged her mount to a canter and loved the movement, the sense of freedom, the feel of the wind on her face, and she soon lost all track of time and distance. She was about to turn round to retrace her route when she heard a voice calling—

"Hey—you there! You're trespassing, young woman," and to her surprise another rider appeared from out of the shadow of a clump of tall trees.

He was a slim man, sitting tall on a high horse, a beautiful gleaming chestnut. Man and mount looked all of a piece, and Karen couldn't help but admire the picture they made as they stood motionless against the tree-line. His riding kit was slightly shabby but well cut, superbly fitted; his boots lovingly polished. He was about twenty-eight or thirty, Karen guessed, and one of the most handsome men she had ever seen. Dark haired, with deep-set dark eyes, an aristocratic-looking nose and chin; his mouth at that moment was set in a firm line, his brow creased with annoyance.

"Don't you know you're trespassing, young lady?" His well-modulated, cultured voice had lost a little of its anger as he returned Karen's interested gaze. She was looking very pretty with her cheeks flushed with embarrassment and the effect of the fresh air and exercise. Her heart was beating a rapid tattoo as she answered apologetically,

"No, I'm sorry. I thought this was still part of the bridle path. I do apologise. You see, I'm new around here."

"You're on Asheby Manor estate now," and from his air of authority, the hauteur in his voice, Karen guessed immediately who this man was, and her back stiffened in the saddle. She had heard a few conflicting reports of the Hon. Simon, hadn't she, but Karen was far too sensible to listen to tittle-tattle.

Now she was meeting the man face to face and her pulse quickened, for whatever she had heard, nothing had prepared her for the sight of him. His dark eyes were watching her intently now with a look of growing admiration in them; a look Karen felt that could be mirrored in her own eyes, for he was certainly a very attractive-looking man.

"Perhaps you wouldn't mind directing me back to Coombe Magna?"

He reined his horse a little nearer, smiling now and that smile did something wonderful to that proud face; softened it, made him seem more approachable, and Karen found herself smiling back warmly.

"I'm Simon Asheby," he introduced himself touching the peak of his riding hat. "Are you one of John's guests?"

"Nothing so illustrious, I'm afraid," she smiled ruefully. "I'm Karen Stevens, the new nurse working for Mr. Lyle-Coombe, that's all."

Simon's smile deepened.

"And I bet you look cute in your uniform, Miss Stevens. Ride a little way further on with me and you can see Asheby Manor from up there. Please forgive me if I seemed annoyed just now, but trespassers are the very devil at times, you know."

As they trotted side by side, they chatted easily. Simon was very interested in Karen's job, and as she told him about it, sometimes seriously, sometimes with amusement, she found they had covered quite a bit of ground. He was so easy to talk to, so interested in all she had to say. As they rode, he pointed out various features of the estate, his voice filled with pride. He certainly loved his inheritance, Karen thought, and she didn't blame him.

"I've already heard a lot about Asheby Manor estate, Mr—er?" She paused—how did one address an Honourable?

"Please call me Simon," he put in easily.

"I believe Asheby Bay once belonged to you, too," she went on, and then paused. His dark brow had creased into a frown and his lips tightened, and she wondered if she had been tactless to remind him of his loss? "I think it was good of you to let my employer have it—it's such an asset;

great for guests to have a little private bay, so safe for the kiddies . . ." she heard her voice babbling on and faltered to a halt.

"I didn't want to part with it, Nurse Stevens, but . . ." he shrugged his slim shoulders and then changed the subject as they reached the brow of the hill. "There it is—and this is my favourite view of it."

Karen could well understand that proud tone in his voice as he pointed with his riding crop. Asheby Manor in the sunlight was indeed a glorious sight. Mellowed stonework, tall twisting chimneys, mullioned windows catching the light; wide sweeping curves of the twin drives leading to a flight of well-worn stone steps —it stood there defying time, mellowing with time, proudly timeless, as if it knew it would always be there, long after other things had been eroded away.

"It *is* beautiful, Simon," Karen breathed slowly. "I don't blame you for loving it so."

He turned to her, studying her face.

"I do. It's the one true love of my life —my beloved burden." And there was something in his voice then that brought a lump to Karen's throat and she knew that whatever others thought about this man, she would always understand his love of Asheby Manor.

"I must be getting back. Thank you for showing me," she said simply.

"You must come and see inside, Karen." She was pleased that he used her first name.

"Well, we start taking the first guests of the season next week, and then my free times will be strictly limited, but I would like to see inside your lovely Manor. And thanks again for letting me trespass."

"You have my permission to ride anywhere, Karen," he replied, "at anytime."

Simon Asheby rode back part of the way with her until she was once more on the right path for Coombe Magna. He stretched across the back of his horse and held out his hand and Karen put hers in it, thrilling at the touch of his firm grip.

"I'll be seeing you again then, Karen," he said.

"I hope so. 'Bye, Simon," and as Karen rode gently back along the bridle path, she could almost feel his eyes still watching her progress, and she told herself she was a fool to let it please her! He was just being kind; his interest had just been a passing thing. After all, she was just working at Coombe Magna, whilst he was the Hon. Simon, owner of the fabulous Asheby Manor.

But that didn't stop her from remembering the way his dark eyes had looked at her, full of admiration, liking what they had seen. According to Dr. Matthew Henshaw, Simon was only concerned with the amount of money he could get for his land, not with the necessity for a Maternity Centre. And yet he hadn't seemed hard and grasping to Karen that morning. She sighed and once more reminded herself that she was here to do a job, not to mix up in local politics! All the same, Simon's dark eyes were constantly before her the next few days . . .

Almost the first guests to arrive the next Monday morning were Mrs. Manning and her daughter, Angela.

"Look here, nurse, I want you personally to see the old lady safely installed in her rooms. They're taking a contained suite in the main house." John Lyle-Coombe looked a bit harassed that morning, his face almost puce-looking and his big desk covered with lists and letters. "They want to stay here for the whole season, so I want everything to be just right for them. Hetty Manning was a friend of my late wife's family and she's not in very good health."

He gave Karen a wry smile, and then went on, "At least, that's what she says; always grumbling about something that's wrong with her every time I see the woman. She can be a bit of a bind, nurse, but I can't afford to offend such good clients, can I?"

"Of course not. I'll take special care of her, Mr. John, don't worry," Karen promised.

"Good. They're having their own place practically pulled down and rebuilt, that's why they're going to stay here—if we make them comfortable enough. She's one of Matthew Henshaw's patients, so he'll be coming in to see her, I suppose. The daughter, Angela is a good-looking wench, so she'll decorate the place nicely," and he gave Karen a mischievous grin, and then added, 'She scares me to death—these glamour gels do . . .'"

And Angela Manning certainly was glamorous. A tall, curvaceous blonde with an extremely haughty manner, and affected smile she didn't bother to use on the domestics, she had the staff running themselves ragged before an hour had passed. Nothing in the pleasant suite was right, and she had two porters moving things around for ages before she agreed to stay.

As for Mrs. Hetty Manning, she complained of so many aches and pains that Karen began to wonder if she had a hypochondriac on her hands, but she would wait and see what the doctor had to tell her.

"I must have my medicines handy, nurse. There . . . no, there, that's it. Do you have a connecting phone to your surgery, nurse? And your own quarters? You do? Oh, good, I may need you in the night; sometimes I just can't sleep for the pain," the whining voice went on as Karen carefully tucked her in to the already prepared bed. The suite wasn't large, but it had a lovely view over the Coombe

Magna grounds, and was well away from the ballroom and games rooms.

"I'm sure you'll be most comfortable here, Mrs. Manning, and with such a lovely view, too. You'll be able to sit out on the little balcony, won't you?" Karen said cheerfully as she settled the heap of pillows.

"It's not too bad, I suppose," came the grudging reply. "Certainly more endurable than our own place at the moment. John told you that we were being done over. . . ?" The old lady was fully prepared to keep the nurse talking there all morning.

"I must go now, Mrs. Manning, my surgery is open and I should be there right now. I think you've everything you need . . ."

"That's what you say, nurse, but I'm sure my heart's playing up—I can feel it beating away like mad," she grumbled, her bony hand clutching her chest convulsively as she groaned.

"Your pulse rate is practically normal, Mrs. Manning. Just try and rest a little while; it's just the effort of getting moved and settled in, you know. Now I must go;

I do hope you have a really pleasant stay here."

As she turned to leave, the daughter, Angela, came into her mother's room.

"Going, nurse? Oh, I thought you might be doing some of mother's unpacking . . ."

Just in time, Karen bit back a sharp retort.

"I'm sorry, Miss Manning, but I'm here for purely nursing duties only, and I'm due at the Medical Unit right now."

Angela Manning looked up from the scarlet-tipped finger nail she had been examining and shrugged, a bored expression marring the beauty of her face.

"Very well; I suppose I'll have to get the chambermaid to do it later," she grumbled, and Karen made her escape.

Phew! that pair were going to be a bit of a nuisance, she grimaced, and then remembering what her employer had said, she straightened her little cap and hurried along the path. She would need all her tact and firmness, but she would have to be careful not to offend either of them.

That was Karen's lesson about the difference between nursing in a general hospital and this job. Here, the customer, guest, patient—call them what you will— was always right. Ah well!

3

THE place was positively buzzing with activity; cars were being unloaded as guests moved in; the girls in Reception were working like mad giving out keys, checking bookings, making hurried notes of the guests' various requirements. Porters and maids were scurrying around frantically. Orders were flying around for early morning tea, for more pillows, extra blankets. Telephone calls were made and answered, luggage lost and found, rooms and bungalows changed at the last moment for some whim or other. The pampered rich definitely took some looking after, Karen told herself whimsically. But by lunch time a good many guests had settled in, changed into holiday clothes and were ready to dine and begin their holiday.

Karen's first few patients were nearly all minor casualties; fingers caught in car doors, grazes, cuts, nose bleeds and bumps; nothing serious she was thankful to record. One of her casualties was a sweet-faced girl named Mavis, who was responsible for all the various flower arrangements around Coombe Magna; she had a nasty septic finger, probably from a rose thorn.

"Sorry, this'll need lancing, pet," Karen told her and seeing the young girl's face drain of its colour, she sat her down and began asking her about her job—chattering away to take the girl's attention from the treatment.

"It's nice to meet you, Mavis, I do so admire your lovely flower arrangements, especially those in the dining-room. Did you have to have much training for your job. . . ?" By the time the finger was duly dressed, the two had become quite friendly, and Mavis's cheeks had regained their normal colour.

"Here you are, pet, a course of antibiotics for you, I'm afraid. And please, call in to see Dr. Henshaw at the next surgery, won't you?"

"Thanks, Karen, you're great . . ." Mavis replied, and left Karen with a glow of pleasure at making another friend.

The next few days were filled with sunshine and enjoyment for the guests; vigorous for some, quiet and restful for others, according to their tastes.

Karen soon noticed that Angela Manning was the focus of attention at the swimming pool and in the ballroom. Her cool, fair beauty and her gorgeous figure were enhanced by the briefest of bikinis, the expensiveness of her lovely dresses. A different one each time, although Karen smiled wryly as she noticed that her bikinis never got wet! Her carefully dressed hair-do was never disturbed! Always surrounded by a crowd of young people; the men especially eyed her with obvious admiration, whilst the girls plainly hated the very sight of her!

She so calmly ordered everyone around that Karen wondered how she ever kept any friends at all, until she noticed that the crowd around her changed constantly. And there were times when the imperious Angela looked positively bored, but she neglected her mother shamefully; leaving her care to the maids and Karen.

The only exception was when Dr. Henshaw was about to make a call . . .

"When Matthew comes in, tell him mother wants to see him, will you?" Without waiting her turn in the waiting-room, Angela pushed her way into Karen's surgery as she was treating a grazed ankle. Karen frowned at the interruption, and then seeing who it was, she replied—

"But the doctor came in especially to see her yesterday, Miss Manning—he has a surgery here today . . ."

Angela shrugged her elegant shoulders.

"Well, mother's not so well today. Besides, I'd like to see him—we're old friends, you know, nurse." The insinuation in her voice made Karen's lips twist wryly. Another of them, she thought; for a struggling young doctor, Dr. Henshaw wasn't doing so badly, what with Lisa Felstead, the cool brunette, and now Angela, the curvaceous blonde!

"Would you like me to see your mother, Miss Manning, if she's not so well?"

"Please yourself," Angela replied care-lessly, "but don't forget to give Matthew my message, will you?"

"I won't, and—er—Miss Manning, I wonder if you would mind—next time, waiting in the waiting-room? This surgery is private to myself and the patient I happen to be seeing at the time. I hope you don't mind?" she finished placatingly.

"Wait in the waiting-room—you must be joking!" Angela exclaimed rudely as she flounced out, slamming the surgery door behind her, and Karen sighed, longing to treat her like the spoilt child she was—with a good spanked bottom!

After surgery she decided to pop in and see Mrs. Manning, although she was pretty certain that a lot of that lady's troubles were in the mind only; she was a typical hypochondriac. Even so, her imagined ailments could possibly be cries for help and that she was trying to gain the attention she quite evidently didn't get from her thoughtless daughter.

As she walked along the path, enjoying the few moments of sunshine on her face, she saw a little girl coming towards her, looking frantically around, her small face pale, her large eyes tragic and worried-looking so that Karen stopped and asked her—

"Lost something, pet?"

The child paused and her thin chest was heaving, her breathing shallow and distressed.

"No, I'm looking for things for the treasure hunt, and I can't find them," and she was almost in tears.

"Well, it's only a game, darling, it doesn't matter if you don't find them all, you know."

"Oh, but Mummy . . . I've just *got* to win this competition today. And it's the first heats of the junior swimming soon, and I'll be late. I've just got to win; Mummy says she's sure I'll win the major award this week! She's going in with Daddy for *all* the grown-ups things; they're ever so good, too."

All too clearly, the picture rose in Karen's mind and she was alarmed at the child's distress. This was awful! And her anger at the foolishness of some stupid parents threatened to overwhelm her usual calm judgment.

"Well, darling . . . what do I call you?"

"Emma."

"Well, Emma, let's see your list, and I'll

help you find some of the treasures, shall I?"

"But that would be cheating, wouldn't it?" the child's clear eyes gazed hopefully up at her face.

"Sort of—but you've heard of 'with a little help from our friends', haven't you, Emma? Well, let me be your friend and help you—just this once, eh?"

So for the next few minutes, Karen helped to find a selection of leaves and flowers, a feather, an empty matchbox, cigarette carton, and then saw a delighted Emma on her way. The little girl was still having trouble with her breathing and Karen hoped her mother had the necessary asthma inhalant with her for she was surely going to need it soon, if she wasn't mistaken!

She found Mrs. Manning surrounded by pillows and rugs, even though the day was fairly warm and the heating turned up high in her apartment.

"Oh, do come in, nurse, I thought it was the doctor . . ." and she lifted a languid, gnarled hand to pat the seat beside her.

"Your daughter tells me you're not so

well, Mrs. Manning. Perhaps I can help you?"

"I doubt it, my dear. Only Dr. Henshaw understands me," she replied off-handedly.

Keeping her face calm and controlled, Karen asked—

"Tell me what's bothering you, Mrs. Manning."

"Oh, everything! My back and neck ache; I've a pain here—and here, and I feel quite sick most of the time."

With a glance at the half-empty box of chocolates on the small table beside her, Karen thought she knew what might be causing the last complaint at least! She picked up a small bottle of tablets, and saw that it contained fairly strong painkillers.

"Did Dr. Henshaw give you these?"

"Of course. I couldn't manage without them, nurse," Mrs. Manning replied sharply.

"Suppose I help you on to the bed. Perhaps you'll feel more comfortable there, Mrs. Manning? Doctor's coming in to see you soon."

"Oh, very well, but I don't feel comfortable even lying down," she grumbled, and for a moment, Karen sympathised with her daughter. It couldn't be much fun having to listen to that perpetual whine all day, could it?

Karen left her lying on the bed, her magazines to hand, the long window, opening out on to the small balcony, propped back.

"You must have some fresh air, Mrs. Manning," she said firmly. "There—that curtain cuts out the glare of the sun, doesn't it? I'll get a pot of tea sent up, shall I?"

And Mrs. Manning, pleased to think she was going to have some attention, some fuss made of her, managed a weak smile in response.

On the way back to the Medical Unit, Karen was surprised to see the broad back of Dr. Henshaw as he stood talking to Angela. In his plain, sober grey suit, he looked rather out of place amidst the colourfully dressed holidaymakers. Angela, as usual, had an expensive matching toga over her bikini, and with her fair hair coiled back on the nape of her slender neck, her long, smooth limbs, she looked like a sun goddess. Her face was full of animation, her big blue eyes raised to the doctor's with obvious disregard for any onlookers, and Karen had to admit to herself that the doctor certainly wasn't in any hurry to go and see his patient.

She bit her lip, loth to interrupt the scene, and yet she couldn't very well walk by to carry on to her quarters when she wanted to see him about Angela's mother, could she? So she turned and slowly retraced her steps to the big house, and not wanting to disturb Mrs. Manning, she waited, kicking her heels in the entrance hall, hoping to catch the doctor when he came in. *When* he came, thought Karen crossly a little later, fed-up with hanging about!

"Ah, there you are, nurse, I was looking for you," he said breezily and Karen almost gasped.

"Yes, I saw you talking to Miss Manning, so I thought I'd wait here. I wanted to see you about her mother. She seems to be in very low spirits, with a certain amount of pain. If you could give me some idea of her medical history, doctor. . . ?"

Karen's voice was cool. A man who

professed to be at loggerheads with rich landowners and yet worked for one; attended a rich widow and played around with her daughter, was not *her* idea of a struggling doctor! Her eyes as she watched the rugged face were distant and cool, and the doctor's eyebrows rose.

"Been giving you a rough time, has she, our Mrs. Manning?"

"Well, shall we say, doctor, that she could keep a full-time private nurse pretty busy with all her ailments—to say nothing of acting as lady's maid to her daughter!"

Matthew Henshaw's eyebrows rose even higher and he said,

"I won't detain you then, nurse. I'll pop in and see you before I go and let you have Mrs. Manning's details . . ." and Karen felt herself to be dismissed.

Her phone was ringing when she got back to the surgery; it was Lisa Felstead with a message for Dr. Henshaw.

"Can I pass it on, Miss Felstead, he will be in here in a few moments?"

"No, thank you, nurse. Please ask doctor to ring me back."

The secretary's voice was so cold and unfriendly that Karen agreed to pass on the request and hung up quickly. A prickly pair, the doctor and his secretary, thought Karen wryly, and she was glad her colleagues in the resort weren't so stand-offish, for she missed the happy co-operation of St. Catherine's very much.

As soon as the doctor came in, he rang through to his surgery, and Karen could hear him laughing and chatting easily enough to Lisa Felstead. But when he came through and perched on the corner of her desk, his manner was strictly professional as they began to discuss Mrs. Manning.

"I do think she has too much time alone —to think about herself, doctor. She needs to lose weight, take more outside exercise, mix a little more with other people. She's on her own quite a lot; her daughter naturally wants to be with younger folks."

"You're quite right, nurse. She had Angela rather late—a difficult confinement. On the face of it, she does seem to imagine many of her troubles. But, nurse, she does have quite a lot of referred pain from her spine. Along with ankylosing spondylitis, she has a certain amount of other arthritis, causing pain of the neck and shoulders, also stiffness in the sacro-iliac joints. I've had X-rays done lately and she should have physiotherapy every day as well as the drugs I've given her. Facilities around here are rather inadequate—even for someone who can afford to pay—as she can."

"Could we arrange for a physiotherapist to come in daily and give her some treatment here? I could help where necessary; it might help to alleviate her pain somewhat?"

Karen was feeling a little ashamed of some of the thoughts she had recently harboured about the patient; it was quite evident she *did* suffer from pain, from what the doctor had just said. Perhaps later, she might be able to get Mrs. Manning to go down to the Sauna for treatment and mix up with others like herself?

"I wonder if I could get her interested in something that would get her out and about a little . . . ?" she mused aloud.

Matt Henshaw's mouth lifted in a crooked smile.

"You'll have your work cut out, nurse,

I reckon, but you could give it a try. Now, how are things here?" he asked looking round the little surgery. "Settling in, are you? Any queries? I'll be in tomorrow for surgery, but if there's anything . . ."

"Nothing I can't handle, doctor, thank you."

"Good, see you tomorrow then," and with that he went, leaving Karen pondering just how good a doctor he was?

However, she sought out Pete and Penny Naylor as soon as she could and explained her problem.

"Anything you can suggest for our Mrs. Manning would be welcome, Penny," Karen begged, but none of them could see that lady joining in the many energetic activities in the resort! Then Pete said suddenly—

"What about cards, Karen? Not the usual school in the card room—no. I wonder if she plays bridge? I could perhaps fix up a quiet little four—make up a table in one of the smaller lounges perhaps?"

"What a good. idea," put in his wife eagerly. "Better still, what about one of the little gazebo things—you know, the little summer houses? There's a couple of them in the grounds; nice and quiet and sunny. Put up a table or so—serve them tea or coffee."

Penny's face was alight with interest, and Karen could see why she was such a success at her job!

That evening, Karen had her first emergency. It happened when most of the guests were dressing for dinner. Karen was going back to her own quarters to clear up for the evening, when a sudden commotion made her pause and then turn to where an anxious group of people were standing looking down in alarm at someone on the ground. An accident? Karen ran across swiftly, shouldering the white-clad tennis players out of the way.

"What's happened?" She knelt down and saw that the young man on the ground was unconscious, his face white and glistening with sweat.

"Too much to drink by the look of him!" a voice behind her muttered. "Been playing tennis all afternoon, then he's been lifting his elbow at the bar, I suppose."

But Karen knew otherwise—this was no drunken stupor. She loosened the young man's clothing, and turned his head on one side. This could either be a coma or a hypoglycaemic attack, but certainly the young man was a diabetic, and a fool to let himself in for such an attack. She felt in the pocket of his shorts, but there were no customary lumps of sugar.

Willing hands carried him to the Medical Unit and Karen got through to the local hospital, asking that an ambulance be sent for him at once.

The receiving ward sister quibbled at the other end; a doctor usually orders an ambulance for an admittance, Karen was told. Curtly, tersely, she ordered them to send the ambulance at once!

"I'll get Dr. Henshaw to confirm this, but meanwhile I have an emergency that needs immediate attention . . . ."

She slammed down the receiver and then lifted it again to ring through to Lisa Felstead, and this time Karen was in no mood to put up with her un-cooperative airs and graces!

"Please get Dr. Henshaw to ring the General Hospital at once and confirm my call, Miss Felstead—at once!" she repeated.

Karen went along to see the patient comfortably installed; he would only need a couple of days in hospital to get him stabilised once more. After that, she would have a few words to say to that young man! As a diabetic, he should have known better than to play tennis all afternoon on an empty stomach. Also she would have. . . to get some sort of working arrangement clearly defined with the hospital, wouldn't she?

The next morning, Karen went in to see Mrs. Manning.

"Just a few moments before surgery," she told her cheerfully. "How are you today, Mrs. Manning?" And after giving the lady a few moments to get through her usual list of moans, she asked casually—

"Do you play bridge at all, Mrs. Manning?"

"Bridge? Why yes, I used to play with my husband as my partner quite a lot. Why?"

"If we could arrange to make up a four, would you like a rubber now and then? There's a nice quiet corner in one of the lounges or, better still, how about one of the summerhouses? Make a lovely little meeting place for four; tea with friends, probably not in your class as players, but . . ." Karen cunningly coaxed, playing on the old lady's vanity.

"Well, I don't know—my back . . ." But Karen could see she was rather pleased with the suggestion.

"Anyway, think about it, Mrs. Manning; I'll tell the hostess to look out for partners, shall I? Probably quite a few would like to play bridge."

Karen found a very worried-looking young mother in the waiting-room when she got back.

"Oh, Nurse Stevens, it's my little girl, Emma . . ." she began, and Karen noticed that her hands were clenched tightly together, her eyes frightened.

"Come through here and tell me."

"Emma—she has asthma occasionally. Has done since she was very small. Last night she seemed rather poorly, and we've been up all night."

"Then why didn't you send for me before—or the doctor?"

"Well, we had our usual tablets with us;

we thought it would pass. It usually does, but this time she seems so poorly."

Leaving a note, Karen hurried with the mother across to their luxurious bungalow. There was a large, expensive-looking car in the car port and quite an amount of sports equipment lying around; obviously Emma's parents were fairly wealthy.

Karen instantly recognised the little girl from the day before—the treasure hunt little girl, so anxiously worried to collect all the clues.

"Hello, Emma, my pet. Not feeling too good this morning?"

The little chest was heaving, the breathing noisy, a distressed child indeed, and Karen fancied she knew why!

"Keep her quiet. I'll have Dr. Henshaw see her the moment he comes in. That'll be . . ." she consulted her watch, "in a very short time now. I must get back to be there, but he won't be long. Don't worry, pet," she told the little girl, "we'll soon have you better again."

Karen felt like reading the riot act to the parents for their behaviour had certainly helped to bring about their daughter's present attack, but she had no time to spare right then. All the same, as she explained the case to the doctor as soon as he came in for surgery, she couldn't help adding—

"This attack has been brought on by stress, doctor. The parents have been pushing Emma too hard this week, wanting her to go in for—and win—all the kiddies' competitions. She's a typical nervous asthmatic, whilst they are the healthy, hearty types who probably can't realise they have a child with this particular weakness. She's pushed too much, worrying herself, trying to please her parents, keeping up with what they expect of her . . ." Karen paused for breath, the pity she felt for little Emma all too plainly written on her open face. Pity and anger at the lack of perception in the child's parents.

"Quite the amateur psychologist, aren't we, nurse?"

Karen caught her breath at the sarcasm in the doctor's remark and her face flushed. No doubt she had perhaps overstepped the mark, but she felt so strongly about all this.

"Thought you should know what I

think, before you go and see Emma. I said you would see her at once, doctor, is that all right? There isn't anything urgent here at the moment." Her voice was composed now, her temper under control, but the sardonic look in Dr. Matthew's brown eyes told her he was aware that his shaft had stung!

The waiting-room, when he returned, held several patients, mostly wanting prescriptions for drugs they had forgotten to bring with them. One of these was an attractive girl in a smart overall—she was the Coombe Magna hairdresser and was always very busy, especially as she went to guests' apartments to do their hair for them. She held out her hands and Karen saw they were covered in an angry red rash, which looked very sore and painful.

"You haven't been using the cream I prescribed, have you, Felice?" Obviously the girl was a regular patient, and her face took on a mutinous look as she answered—

"Of course not! How can I in my job? No sooner have I smeared it on than I have my hands in water and shampoo again!"

Seeing the frown on the doctor's face, Karen asked—

"Have you changed your brand of shampoo, or setting lotion or anything else lately, Felice?"

"Nothing. No, nothing at all," the girl replied emphatically.

"How about working in rubber gloves then?" Matt Henshaw suggested, looking a little lost when it came to discussing cosmetics.

"I do, as much as I can, but I can't use them when I'm putting in hair rollers and so on. Besides," she said truculently, "the rubber gloves seem to make them itch even worse and . . ."

"What about those gloves?" Karen put in quickly. 'Using a different brand?"

The girl's face lightened.

"Oh, yes. Actually, I'm using some thinner ones—cheaper, too. I seem to get through such a lot." She nodded, adding, "These came from Hong Kong, I wonder . . ."

"Could be something about them that's causing the trouble then. Go back to your old brand and see, will you, Felice?" the doctor said, "and use the cream whenever you can, there's a good girl."

After checking a couple of bad sprains that Karen wanted him to see, he washed his hands as the final patient left, and as he turned from the washbasin, he looked across at her quizzically.

"You were right, nurse. A wee chat with young Emma put me in the picture. She needs to have some more tablets with her; I've also handed out a polite ticking-off to those stupid clots she's lumbered with as parents! Some people never ought to have children."

Karen wondered whether his heated words covered an admission that she had been right? Was he trying to apologise a little for his sarcastic remark? She shrugged; as long as the pressure was eased off little Emma, that was all she was bothered about.

"If she gets worse, nurse, I'll give her an injection. I'll leave some capsules at my surgery—can you pick them up?"

As he dried his hands, he told Karen what he wanted her to do, and then added.

"No coffee, nurse?"

"Have you time?" she asked, as if

surprised, and his answering grin angered her further.

"So—you like it here?" he asked conversationally as they sipped the hot coffee.

"I like Coombe Magna—yes," she replied coolly, hoping he got the inference that outside of Coombe Magna—well . . .

Apparently he did, for to her discomfort, he remarked casually—

"I hear you lost no time in getting acquainted with the Hon. Simon Asheby, did you, nurse? Don't lose your heart in that direction though; that young man will have to marry wealth and position unless I'm mistaken."

Karen's breath caught in her throat; of all the cheek!

"Whereas you'll not have that problem with the fair Angela, will you, Dr. Henshaw—*she* has plenty of money, hasn't she?"

His eyes widened at that, and Karen couldn't help noticing his long, thick lashes—such a waste on a man, the illogical thought flashed through her mind, even as she waited for his reprimand. This time she'd really gone too far, hadn't she?

She stood there, her face crimson, her chin stubborn, awaiting the lash of his tongue. To her surprise, he smiled—a broad smile at first that crinkled the corners of his brown eyes, creased his face into deep laughter lines—and then a louder, heartier peal of laughter.

"Touché, my dear Karen. You're so easy to rile, in spite of your cool and competent exterior! So the Hon. Simon's got a champion, has he? Well, I wish you well, but again I'm warning you. Don't expect a wedding ring from him!"

At those last words, Karen suddenly remembered Keith, and the awful mistake she'd made there; thankful that this infuriating doctor didn't know about *him* at least!

"I'm here to do a job, doctor, not to look for a husband. And if I were, I wouldn't need any advice from someone like—like . . . Now, if you've finished surgery?" she asked coldly.

But he only gave that wide grin of his again as he picked up his bag.

"Be seeing you, Karen . . ."

And for the rest of the day, Karen simmered every time she remembered that morning and wondered why, too, she kept remembering that he had called her Karen instead of Nurse Stevens. . . ?

4

WHEN Karen called at the doctor's surgery the next day to pick up the capsules for Emma, she made her way immediately to Lisa Felstead's small reception desk, and after a brief greeting told her what she wanted.

"*I* can get any further prescriptions signed, nurse, and save you bothering the doctor. He's very busy right now working on his campaign for a new Maternity Centre here. Er—perhaps you'd like to take some of these leaflets explaining all about it? After all, you do have some wealthy clients at Coombe Magna, don't you?"

Karen hesitated, trying to choose the right words.

"I'm sorry, but I don't think I should. I don't know Mr. Lyle-Coombe's views on the matter, and as I work for him . . ."

Lisa Felstead's dark eyebrows rose like two question marks.

"But surely you agree with the need for

such a centre, nurse? You, of all people, should support the doctor's campaign, even if some of the ignorant folks around here can't see the necessity!"

Conscious of the fact that several of those same local people were sitting listening to the secretary's every word, Karen murmured quietly—

"I'm new to the district, Miss Felstead, and so for the moment I must refrain from getting involved in local affairs . . ." and seeing that the other girl was about to interrupt, she added quickly, ". . . until I've heard both sides of the question, that is. Be seeing you, Miss Felstead," and with that, Karen took her leave.

So that's how the wind blows, is it, she thought? The aloof Miss Felstead certainly wears her heart on her sleeve when it comes to Dr. Matthew Henshaw! So, of course, she would be on his side when it concerned the fight for the new Maternity Centre. From a purely professional view, Karen was too. A well-equipped, well-staffed centre where doctors and specialists had the support and back-up of the latest instruments, competent records and so on —yes, any sensible caring nurse and midwife would wish for that. But Karen was not at all sure that Dr. Henshaw was going about getting it in the right way.

According to him, Simon Asheby was some sort of grasping monster, unconcerned with the needs of others less fortunate than himself, and yet he hadn't struck Karen as being completely heartless and hard when she'd met him the other day.

She had also heard that the local mothers were almost superstitiously fond of their old maternity wing, and didn't want it pulled down.

She had a little time yet before she had to return to Coombe Magna and relieve Mrs. Roberts, and the sunshine was tempting. She strolled slowly towards the tiny harbour, watching the boats bobbing gently with the swell of the tide. It was a pretty sight, and the air was clean and fresh, although it did carry the odours of a small fishing port. Tarred ropes coiled around bollards linking the smaller craft, and here and there she could see the sleek trim lines of power boats and small yachts.

"Hello there, Nurse Stevens— Karen . . ." She turned at the sound of her name and her face flushed with pleasure at the sight of the tall, slim figure of a man coming towards her. It was Simon Asheby, dressed casually in faded jeans and an old sailing sweater.

"I thought I recognised you. Off duty?"

"Only for a little while," Karen smiled warmly up into his blue eyes with unfeigned pleasure. "This is the first time I've seen the harbour," she added, surprised by the rapid beat of her heart against her ribs. "Do you have a boat here, Simon?" she asked and hoped he didn't notice the tremor in her voice.

"Yes. There she is, over there," he pointed to a long, light power craft swaying gently at the private mooring to their left. "Lillane—named after my mother. She's a nice little thing—the boat, I mean, not . . ." he paused and then asked, "Have you time for a cup of tea, Karen?"

She nodded, brown eyes alight with pleasure.

"I'd love one, thanks," and in no time at all, they were seated at a small table in a quiet tearoom away from the harbour. Simon was evidently well known, for an elderly waitress came over to take his order immediately.

"Hello, Meg. Any of your delicious scones ready?"

"Oh yes, sir. Pot of tea for two?" She beamed at him in such a friendly way that, when she left to fetch the order, Simon told Karen by way of explanation—

"Meg was a parlour maid with us for years, but we had to let her go." There was a hint of regret in his voice that Karen was quick to notice.

"I suppose it's hard to keep staff, isn't it?"

For a moment, Simon looked pensively at her open face, and then, as if he had come to some decision, he said—

"We—I can't afford to keep staff, Karen." She waited for him to go on. "You see, my father, well—he wasn't very good with money; allowed himself to be robbed; made foolish investments, and when he died there were heavy death duties to be paid. Things have gone from bad to worse and no matter how hard I work, I'm afraid that one day I'll lose Asheby Manor and its estates. We had to sell one or two of the outlying farms to meet the death duties, and then more recently, we sold John the small bay he wanted to open his place as a holiday complex."

Deeply interested, Karen watched the play of emotions on the proud, good-looking face. He gave a wry, twisted smile that curved his mouth, but didn't quite reach those blue eyes.

"It's damned hard these days being the owner of an old estate; there's plenty of land, but that needs cash to upkeep it, plenty of responsibilities—wages, repairs, taxes . . ." he shrugged as Meg brought their tea.

"I shouldn't be telling you all this, Karen, I'm sure it's of no interest to you," he finished with a smile.

"Oh, but it is. I can see how dearly you must love Asheby Manor. It must be awful to have to sell bits and pieces of your estate. I don't blame you in the least for wanting to hold on to it; to want to pass it on to your children one day."

She paused, spreading the hot scone liberally with butter.

"Have you any brothers or sisters, Simon?"

"An elder brother," he grimaced. "We've had no contact for years, and my mother's not in very good health; hasn't been since father died. The trouble is, Karen, she simply doesn't, or won't, understand how things have changed. She still lives, bless her, in the past when there was money enough for everything. She still orders things I can't afford to pay for; still grumbles about lack of servants, and parties, and travel abroad—all that kind of thing. Father used to indulge her every whim," he said ruefully, "hence the pile of debts when he died."

"Have you tried to make her understand, Simon? After all, she must be a fairly intelligent woman."

"Well, I'm afraid to, I suppose. Her heart's none too good, and she seems to get so upset at the thought of losing Asheby."

Without thinking, Karen reached out her hand and touched Simon's as it lay on the table and gave it a sympathetic squeeze.

"I'm so sorry, Simon, it can't be easy for you."

A flash of warmth crossed his blue eyes and he returned the pressure.

"Look, Karen, I don't want any of this to get around," and as she made to demur, he hurried on, "Of course, most people around here know there's not too much cash now in our family, but as yet, my credit's good, and so . . ."

"Please, Simon, I won't say anything. Thanks for telling me. After all, we've only recently met, but I honestly do sympathise with you. I'd simply hate to have to sell my inheritance if I were in your shoes."

"I wish everyone felt as you do, Karen. All others can see is a large amount of ground that could be used for all their various wants, but I'm determined to fight tooth and nail for every inch. They all want to take the best bits—our access to the roads, to the sea; to eat away and leave us without any privacy . . ." Simon's deep voice was full of passion as he explained how he felt about the beloved estate.

Then, as if trying to change the subject deliberately, he started to ask Karen about her job, his proud face softening as he watched her mouth curve into laughter as she responded to his charm. If only others could see behind his arrogant bearing, she thought. If only Dr. Henshaw knew Simon's side of the problem, surely he would think differently, understand how the owner of Asheby felt? But she had just promised Simon not to discuss his affairs with anyone else, hadn't she? And she meant to keep that promise.

Besides, she thought perversely, why should she enlighten the confident Dr. Henshaw? He was *so* sure that he was in the right, so did his secretary, the cool efficient Miss Felstead. Why should she tell them that they could just be wrong in thinking Simon Asheby to be hard and grasping? Oh yes, she mused, as she sat there that afternoon, there were always two sides to any conflict!

"Don't forget you're coming up to see inside the Manor, will you, Karen? It's been great talking to you like this— someone from outside the tight local circle can often see things so much more clearly. Besides," he finished with a warm smile, "it's done me good to have a moan to a pretty girl like you, without boring her to tears."

Karen found her heart lifting with pleasure at the admiration in Simon's eyes.

"When are you free again, Karen?" he persisted.

She told him, adding,

"But I shall have to be back for the evening surgery. Dr. Henshaw comes in twice a week, you see."

At the mention of the doctor's name, Simon's brow creased into a deep frown, and to Karen's dismay, there was a feeling of distinct coolness in his next words.

"Ah, Dr. Henshaw's your colleague, is he? Well, he's no friend of mine. He's doing his damnedest to blacken my name lately. He wants a piece of land that would curtail Asheby Manor's rear access, and wants me to practically give it to him, too. Well, I can't, Karen! I would need to get a good price for *any* bit of land I'm forced to sell, and that piece especially." He passed his hand across his chin, looking at her closely. "I do hope he doesn't persuade you into thinking me an avaricious landowner, Karen, my dear?"

And at the entreaty in his voice, her heart lurched and then went on thudding loudly. So loudly, that surely he must hear it?

"I think for myself, Simon," she said firmly. "Please don't let the fact that I have to work with Matthew Henshaw make things . . . well, I would like to come and see inside your home, Simon," she said softly.

And so it was arranged, and as Karen hurried back to Coombe Magna, her mind was in a turmoil. She could honestly see Matthew Henshaw's burning ambition for what it truly was, but she could also understand Simon's reluctance to part with his land, too.

She sighed deeply as she changed into her white uniform dress and cap; she hoped she would not be caught between the two sides.

She went across to see how Emma was getting on and found a pair of very subdued parents.

"It was our fault, nurse. We knew that any stress brought on Emma's asthma, but I suppose we simply got carried away, being on holiday. She's so shy really and needs pushing a little," the young mother explained, really upset for her thought-lessness.

"Emma will possibly grow out of this, so please don't worry or let her see you worrying, will you? Let her make her own pace. Swimming is good for her, or anything else that makes her breathe deeply, but stress and competition—no. She's so much better today; I should take her down to the beach—let her build a sandcastle and have a little paddle, eh?"

Karen's quiet words did much to reassure the worried mother, and she hoped all would be well now for little Emma.

All was evidently not well with a chum of young Ricky's. She found the two of them waiting for her outside the Medical Unit.

"I told him, nurse, he'd better let you see his knee. It's bleeding something awful —look . . ."

Full of importance, Ricky ushered his friend into the surgery.

"This is Luke Martin, nurse. His mother's a famous film star, an' he's got a smashing new BMX bike."

Karen removed a rather grubby

handkerchief from the other lad's knee. He was taller, more solid-looking than Ricky; unhealthily overweight, her first glance told her as she cleansed the wound.

"Hey, that hurts!" Luke's yell made Ricky look at him in disgust.

"Sorry, Luke, but that's a nasty graze and I must clean it up a bit." Karen's firm touch was as gentle as she could make it.

"Stop it—leave me alone, it hurts . . ." the older boy squirmed, pushing away the swab in Karen's fingers.

"Come on, Luke, don't be a big baby. There you are; now for a cleaning dressing and you'll be fine."

"I'll tell my mother about you, nurse, for hurting me, and you'll cop it, you'll see."

What a horrible child! Ricky's large brown eyes looked across at her apologetically and he raised his thin shoulders.

"These rich kids!" he muttered and then thanked her, pushing the still complaining Luke out before him as he did so. "See you later, nurse," he promised.

Not the sort of friend for young Ricky, Karen mused as she cleared up. She definitely hadn't taken to the pasty-faced Luke, with his small, shifty eyes. Making an entry in her case book, she found a note asking her to call at one of the most expensive bungalows in Coombe Magna occupied by a family who had arrived only the day before.

To her dismay, Karen found two of the family—the father and a young child—looking very poorly indeed.

"They've been fetching up all night, nurse, with dreadful diarrhoea. The poor maid's been in and out all the time."

Carefully, Karen examined the patients; both had stomach pains, headaches and a slight rise in temperature. Scrubbing her hands, she turned to the mother, Mrs. Parker-Smith.

"Did you eat on the way up here, Mrs. Parker-Smith?"

"Why, yes, we did," she replied wearily.

"The same food—all of you? I mean the same dishes?"

"Well, let me see. No, I had a salad; two others had omelettes. My husband and Junior had the meat pie. Why, what is it, nurse?"

"I think it's food poisoning. There could have been salmonella in the meat pie those two ate," Karen answered briefly. "I'll be back . . ."

Outside the bungalow, Karen drew a deep breath, hoping she was right; that if this was food poisoning, the victims had got it from food eaten before they arrived at Coombe Magna. The greatest scourge of any place like this would be that of mass food poisoning. For the moment, she would have to keep what she suspected very quiet.

She hurried back to the Medical Unit; she knew that if she was right and it was a case of salmonella poisoning, it would take up to about four days to run its course. Returning to the bungalow, she gave the tired mother some powdered kaolin.

"A dessertspoonful in water every four hours, Mrs. Parker-Smith, with plenty of glucose drinks and weak tea. Later, when they feel up to it, we'll give them milk foods and soups; no solids for a few days, eh?" She gave the distracted mother a comforting smile, and told her to keep her hands well-scrubbed.

"And please, don't worry, it will pass. Such a pity though to start your holiday like this, isn't it? I would be most grateful if you would please keep this to yourself; we can't have the rest of Coombe Magna alarmed, can we?"

It took all Karen's practical persuasion to get her to agree to having their meals sent across to the bungalow for a day or two. She didn't want to take any risks, and meanwhile, she would be keeping a wary eye open for any other guests showing similar symptoms.

"I'll get the doctor to look in and also give you a maid to yourselves. Please contact me if you are at all worried; it often seems worse than it really is—let's hope they only have a mild dose . . ."

Karen then went to report to John Lyle-Coombe, who looked worriedly across at her at the news, an anxious frown on his usually cheerful face.

"Can you handle it, nurse? Yes—I'm sorry, my dear, of course you can." He rose from the big desk, pulling his ear—a habit Karen had noticed before. "Let's hope to goodness this doesn't spread, it could ruin me."

"I'm sure it was the food they ate before they got here, Mr. John. Have I your permission to have a look round the kitchens; do a spot check? Don't worry, I'll be discreet. We don't want to start a panic over what may turn out to be a mild attack, anyway," Karen told him.

"Hope you are right. Yes, go anywhere you like, but don't upset my chef though. Let me know of any further developments, nurse."

"I will, and please don't worry. I've handled cases of salmonella before." Her voice was confident and reassuring.

All the same, as she strolled through the busy, hot, steamy kitchens, her eyes were keenly taking in everything. But they were spotlessly clean, with no trace of mice-droppings—another scourge of the mass caterer; there were no signs of meat left lying around half-cooked. Ricky's father, Chef Williams, his face glistening with the heat, his round head topped by a tall, white hat, a large ladle in his hand, turned to watch her progress suspiciously.

"It's all right, Mr. Williams. Just having a little check-up; it's part of my job, you know, and I must earn my pay."

"Just keep out of my way, nurse, and watch yourself on those hot ovens, that's all," he grumbled good-naturedly.

Karen left the kitchens, glad to escape the heat and bustle. Now for the pool . . .

Old Rogers was one of the groundsmen who had worked all his life on the Coombe Magna estate. He was one of the old school, now almost crippled with rheumatism which made him bad-tempered at times. He wasn't too keen on "them there pools" and eyed the scantily-clad figures with disgust. Karen took a sample of the water, meaning to ask Matt Henshaw to get it analysed as soon as he could. The bottom of the pool was not too clean, she reckoned.

"Has the pool been emptied again lately, Mr. Rogers?" she asked the old man carefully after she had tracked him down to the stables where he sat reading the latest racing news.

"'Course it has," he replied truculently. "Why're you asking?"

"Just checking. Hygiene's my job, you know."

"An' that there pool's mine, so mind your own business, my gel."

"Fair enough, Mr. Rogers, but the Health people do spot checks, and we don't want to get Mr. John into trouble, do we?"

She paid several calls that day on the weak and languid couple of patients in the Parker-Smith bungalow; the attack was running its usual course, leaving its victims exhausted and miserable. She arranged to have an extra TV set and more magazines sent in and hoped they would relieve their tedium.

Later, she caught sight of young Ricky as he hurried round towards the rear of the kitchens.

"Hey—what's the matter with your face?" She caught hold of his tee shirt as he tried to wriggle away. His left eye was swollen and discoloured, and there were several scratches on his cheeks. "You've been fighting, haven't you, Ricky? Come on, tell me—I thought we were mates."

Scuffing his feet, head hanging down, he muttered—

"Well, he was taking the eggs out of the nest . . ."

"Who was?"

"That there Luke Martin. So I hit him!"

"And he hit you, too, by the look of things. Oh Ricky, he's much bigger than you." Karen eyed the disconsolate figure fondly, knowing how much he loved the wild life around the estate. "Come on, I've got something that'll soothe your eye."

As she applied a pad to the discoloured eye, he chatted about the other boy, child-like giving away more than he realised. The film star mother was very much married, but Luke had never had a permanent father to discipline him. He was growing up thinking money could buy everything, and was, as far as she could tell, becoming a thoroughly dislikable character. But for some reason, young Ricky felt sorry for him, and was bent on staying his friend.

"Well, all I can say, young lad, is—don't pick too many fights with him—he's too big!"

Mrs. Manning was full of the arrangements that had been made for her and three others to play bridge, and Karen, insisting that a special straight-backed

114

chair was put out for her, asked her if she would let a physiotherapist come in to treat her.

"I don't mind, my dear, but it doesn't do me much good," but Karen could see that she was pleased at the extra attention she was getting. "I'd rather have my own heat lamp from home though, nurse; I don't really trust any other."

"Well, that's all right. I wonder if your daughter would pop home and bring it here, and we'll fix up a daily session for you?" Karen told her cheerfully. She was pleased at the trouble Penny and Pete Naylor had taken, and Mrs. Manning seemed much brighter.

Now to find Angela, she thought, as she left Mrs. Manning happily considering what she would wear for her first bridge session. But as soon as she got outside the main house, Karen found that she was wanted urgently. A little boy had got his head stuck through some railings, and everyone was in a panic because it wouldn't come out again! Karen suppressed the smile that rose to her lips —never a dull moment, was there? Collecting some butter from the kitchens, she hurried to where a small crowd of spectators was giving the weeping child lots of advice and help—most of it useless! The eyes trying to see her were terrified, and his small neck and ears were red with the pushing and pulling.

Gently, Karen knelt down to calm the frightened little boy; soothingly, softly, she told him—

"Don't worry, darling, we'll have you out in no time. If your head went through —then it'll come out again, won't it? Stands to reason. Now—we just put some butter on the railings like this . . . and then we lift you up, turn you over like this . . . and there—you're free again. Okay?"

Hiccuping loudly, sniffling to stifle his sobs, the little boy looked up at her in awe, while his frantic mother thanked her over and over again between berating her adventurous child.

"Won't some other time do, nurse? I want to get my hair done for the dance tonight. Besides, there's several heat lamps in that sauna place; can't you use one of those?" Angela Manning wasn't at all pleased when

Karen asked her if she would kindly fetch her mother's lamp from their home.

"I'm sorry, but it seems she will only use her own—says she's frightened of those we have here. And I would like one here for use first thing in the morning, Miss Manning, if you could get it?"

"Oh, very well, I'll take the car. No need to change," Angela replied grudgingly.

Karen was scrubbing her hands free of the last of the butter and dirt, gazing dreamily out of the window, hoping she had finished with emergencies for the day. It had been an eventful, busy day, almost as busy as Casualty at St. Catherine's, but here there was only one pair of hands to cope and then clear away and clean up afterwards.

Suddenly, to her horror, there was a scream of brakes, a grinding of tyres on tarmac and the crash of metal and splintering glass! Without waiting to finish drying her hands, Karen snatched up her bag and ran. Ran through the rear entrance to Coombe Magna to see what had caused that terrible noise. Two cars, crushed and jammed together, wheels still revolving, windows shattered, stalled engines still labouring sluggishly, told their own tale. Sightseers began gathering from everywhere, muttering curiously, shoving and pushing.

To Karen's dismay, she saw that one of the cars—a low, long powerful sports car —belonged to Angela Manning, and even as her eyes took in the fact, she saw the tall blonde girl clamber through the crumpled door, staggering and dazed.

There was no movement from the other car, and Karen ran across to peer inside. The driver—a man—was slumped over the wheel, glass from the windscreen covering the front of him. And Karen's experienced eye took in one dreadful fact —that somewhere there was a severed artery. She could tell from the spurts, quick, bright scarlet jets of life blood, that hit the roof of the car and then covered the front of her white dress.

For one brief moment, Karen felt the normal panic that a severed artery brings, and then her quick fingers were seeking, feeling for the spot. The man's left wrist had been deeply cut by a shard of glass, and Karen . . . thanked heavens for her clean strong fingers and thumb! She pressed and pressed until the spurting, gushing flow had ceased. With her other hand she felt along the groove in the man's upper arm, grateful that he was wearing a short-sleeved cotton tee shirt, and again she pressed hard against the humerus, controlling the haemorrhage.

It seemed ages—years, as she crouched there, her back bent in an awkward position; her fingers growing numb with the effort needed. Behind her, she could hear the comments, the helpful suggestions. But thank heavens someone had sent for an ambulance. Then it was a familiar voice behind her that said—

"I'll take over, Karen. Now then—ready . . ."

Karen's back almost refused to straighten as her fingers slipped first off the wrist and then the biceps. Swiftly, with cool precision, Matt Henshaw bound the wrist and applied a tourniquet to the man's upper arm. The man would probably need a blood transfusion.

As the ambulance turned for the hospital, Karen saw the doctor gently tending the weeping, shocked Angela.

"He came straight at me," the blonde girl sobbed. "He never even saw me—he might have killed me . . ."

"Come on, get into my car, I'll run you up to Coombe Magna house. You, too, nurse, she'll need you."

To Karen's surprise, as she clambered into the back of the doctor's car, she saw that Lisa Felstead was already in there. Angela was crying loudly, blaming the other driver, frightened and shocked to the core.

"It wasn't my fault," she repeated over and over.

"Where's your shoes, Miss Manning?" Karen's voice broke through the other girl's sobs.

"Shoes? Oh, in the car—my wedge sandals—I kicked them off," Angela answered.

"So you were driving bare-footed then? And you drive very fast in that car of yours, too?" Karen could scarcely conceal her accusation. The man in the other car could have died; he probably had other injuries as well.

How like Angela Manning to dash out to her car, kick off her clogs and try to drive bare-footed. What control could she possibly have in that monster of a sports car? Karen asked herself angrily. Suddenly, Angela realised what Karen was getting at, and she started to cry afresh, with loud pathetic sobs.

"Stop it, Angela, my dear, you're not badly hurt. I'm sure you couldn't help it. Here we are. Help her to her room, nurse, will you? See if there are any injuries. I'll be back in a moment. Come with me, Lisa . . ."

Karen was thankful that Angela's mother wasn't in; glad of the game of bridge that had taken her out for once.

She bathed Angela's cuts and got her into bed. She was still trembling with shock, but otherwise unhurt and still beautiful in her distress. Karen had managed to cover the front of her blood-stained dress with a large bath towel, certain it would upset the shocked girl even more. She was sorry for her outburst in the car, but as a nurse she had served on Casualty and she deplored careless driving above all else. She would have thought that applied to a doctor, too, but evidently not to one who was half infatuated by a rich blonde, she thought angrily.

Matt Henshaw and Lisa Felstead came in, talking together.

"The police are measuring up down there . . ."

He examined Angela carefully and gave her a shot in the arm, staying by her side until it took effect, while Karen went back to the surgery, wondering who was doing the same for the injured man.

When he returned with Lisa Felstead by his side, she turned and looked at him, and as if he could read her mind, he told her—

"He's going to be okay, nurse, though the hospital tells me he'd been drinking."

"And that excuses Angela's mad driving, I suppose," she answered sharply.

Standing there beside her, Karen felt Lisa Felstead move, but she was past caring.

"The police have measured the skid marks, Nurse Stevens," Matt Henshaw said coolly. "It looks as if it was his fault, and there are a couple of witnesses who agree that he came round the corner on the wrong side at a hell of a pace."

There was a polite snort from the secretary, and Karen felt her face grow red. She had been wrong, hadn't she?

"I'm sorry—I'm sorry, doctor. I just hated the thought of Miss Manning getting away with it—just because she's a pretty girl—I mean . . ." she stammered in confusion. And this wasn't helped by the obvious enjoyment Lisa Felstead was deriving from her discomfort.

"I know quite well what you were thinking, nurse." Dr. Henshaw's rugged face held a lopsided smile that made Karen's anger rise again. She had been wrong, and she had apologised in front of the superior-looking secretary, too! What more did he want?

She bit her lip, feeling very tired and exhausted from the effect of delayed shock. She straightened her aching back and squared her chin, and then knew that his eyes were watching her closely.

"You did a good job there, Karen, on that artery." The words were gentle, and she suddenly felt the sting of hot tears behind her eyelids. She blinked them away; she was wrong about so many things . . .

"Your face is dirty, nurse," he finished drily, and at that, her temper rose again.

"I'll go and wash and change then, doctor. Miss Manning will sleep now for quite a while, won't she?" Collecting several soiled things, she flounced out of the surgery, leaving Matthew and Miss Felstead together.

Blast Matthew Henshaw, he had a way of making her feel always in the wrong— he and his adoring shadow, the dark Lisa.

It was as she was preparing for bed much later that night that she remembered that she hadn't told him about the two cases of food poisoning, or handed over the sample of pool water to be analysed.

The next morning, she rang the doctors' surgery early before things got busy. Lisa Felstead's voice was offhandedly distant, almost to the point of rudeness, and Karen felt she would quickly lose her temper if she didn't watch herself!

Clearly the other girl had no intention of ever becoming more friendly and helpful, so Karen decided that her best policy would be to steer clear of her as much as possible. The trouble was that she, Karen, could only contact Dr. Henshaw through his secretary. So, as calmly as she could, she asked her to tell the doctor about the two food poisoning cases. Fortunately, as yet there seemed to be no further victims in the resort, so Karen's initial diagnosis had been correct —the Parker-Smiths had been infected elsewhere.

"Please see that Dr. Henshaw knows about these two cases, will you, Miss Felstead, also that I would like a test of the bathing pool water done regularly."

"You can contact the county Medical Officer of Health about that yourself, Nurse Stevens. Dr. Henshaw is far too busy to run errands for you," came the sarcastic remark.

At that, Karen had to bite her lips to restrain her rising temper.

"Miss Felstead—please pass on my message, will you?" And being only human, Karen couldn't help but slam down the receiver with a bang which she hoped would hurt the secretary's ears!

5

MRS. MANNING was finally started on her daily physiotherapy; it would be quite an expensive business having someone come in each day to do it, but she didn't seem to be short of money.

Angela, looking pale and interesting, was disporting herself round the pool, wallowing in the sympathy of her friends there. She had them fetching and carrying for her all that next day. When Karen went over and asked her how she felt, she replied languidly—

"How do you expect me to feel, nurse, when that drunken fool almost killed me? Oh yes," she sneered, "I know you thought it was my fault, didn't you, but of course Matthew knew better. In any case, he would always take my side. We've been —er, close friends ever since he came here."

Karen longed to wipe that smug smile from the lovely face. Just in time, she bit back the retort—"Well, you two deserve each other". Instead, she replied quietly—

"Well, let me know, Miss Manning, if you need any further dressings on those scratches of yours, will you?"

Angela shrugged a slim shoulder, her lips curled.

"I'm sure Matthew will see to those, thank you, nurse," and she turned to speak to a friend near by, dismissing Karen as if she was just a nuisance . . .

Tightening her soft lips against the rising anger, Karen turned away, murmuring—

"Very well, Miss Manning," and she slowly walked along the path towards the Medical Centre, breathing deeply, allowing the sunshine to ease her turmoil. As she passed a wooden seat, she couldn't help noticing the young girl slumped there; she looked so desperately unhappy. And at a second glance, Karen saw that she had been crying. Her face was blotched, her eyes red and swollen.

In spite of the rebuff she had just received at the hands of the insolent Miss Manning, Karen *had* to stop and ask gently,

"Is there anything . . . can I help you, pet?"

Dumbly, the young girl raised her tear-drenched eyes, and shook her head and then turned away from Karen's kindly gaze.

"Please—can't you let me help you? You look so . . ."

"No! No, there's nothing you can do." The girl's voice was soft and sweet. "Nothing anyone can do really."

"Sometimes it helps to talk—even to strangers, you know," Karen persisted softly.

The girl straightened up as if she might just change her mind, and Karen added—

"Why not walk with me back to my little place? I'm ready for a cup of coffee —why not join me?"

For a moment it looked as though the girl was about to refuse, but probably something she saw in the look of kindly concern on Karen's face persuaded her. She rose, saying—

"All right. I've got nothing better to do," and the nurse's heart ached at the despondent note in her voice.

Before they had reached the Medical

Unit Karen had skilfully discovered that the girl was Joanne Thorpe, daughter of C. C. Thorpe . . .

"The famous author?" Karen breathed. "Is he here?"

"Yes, we're here for a month, while he does some research for a new book," the dead-pan voice sounded as if it was a prison sentence!

"Aren't you enjoying Coombe Magna, Joanne? It's a lovely place—plenty of young folks."

"Tell my father that," came the bitter reply, "he hardly lets me out of his sight."

As Karen made two mugs of coffee, it all came tumbling out. Motherless, the unhappy girl was kept almost isolated from youngsters of her own age. She seemed to be at her father's beck and call, and to Karen he sounded like the worst kind of Victorian father! But as usual, her sensible reasoning told her that there were always two sides to any conflict; perhaps he was only an extra caring parent.

As she sipped her coffee, she resolved to try and see the famous C. C. Thorpe for herself—perhaps there was something she could do to help? For the unhappy girl before her now certainly needed cheering up.

"What do you like doing, Joanne? Keen on any sport, games, dancing?"

The other girl shook her head, her heavy hair a swinging curtain almost covering her young face.

"I'm not very good . . . not used to mixing, you see." She paused, her eyes begging Karen's understanding. "I like to swim," she added.

"Well, that's great. We have a smashing pool here," Karen began, and then remembering the boisterous, glamorous crowd that gathered there, she knew it wasn't this shy, timid girl's scene.

"What about the sea? Oh, I know it's not warm enough yet, but—say, what about learning to swim underwater? You know—snorkelling in a wet suit thing, they're doing that already. There's a private bay and a very competent instructor, I'm told."

Some of Karen's enthusiasm seemed to rub off on to Joanne, and her eyes came alight with interest. And so it was arranged. Karen would look out for Joanne and C. C. Thorpe; make herself known and suggest snorkelling lessons, and hope he was agreeable.

"I'll see the instructor . . ." and seeing the look of doubt and uncertainty return to the young girl's face, she added, "Don't worry, you can have lessons on your own, when there's no one else around. Okay?"

They sat chatting together for quite a while until Joanne glanced anxiously at the expensive watch on her slender wrist.

"Oh, I must go—Dad'll be so cross . . ." and with a breathless goodbye, she hurriedly left.

Could he really be such an ogre; he was certainly a very famous author . . .

From then on, it was a very busy morning and Karen was kept busy treating cuts and grazes and stings as first one holiday-maker and then another drifted in and out. As she was clearing up after the final patient, the phone rang on her desk. It was Simon Asheby.

"Is that you, Karen? Simon Asheby here; how about this afternoon, are you still free?"

"Yes, I am, as long as I'm here for the doctor's surgery session this evening."

"Good. Ride over and I'll meet you on

the hill. I've told Mother I'm bringing you over for tea and to meet her. Okay?"

"I'd love that. Thank you, Simon, see you later then."

And Karen's heart was light as she finished clearing up the surgery, filling in the case book and leaving everything ready for Mrs. Roberts to take over. As soon after lunch as she could, Karen changed into a pair of fawn-coloured trousers—the nearest thing she had to jodhpurs with her —and a thin cotton polo-necked sweater, and went out to saddle up Brown Belle. The gentle mare whinnied softly as Karen stroked her glossy neck; they both looked forward with pleasure to the afternoon's canter.

It was good to be away from the resort for a while. Comfortable, select and pleasant as it was, there was always a great deal of activity going on and Karen was glad to have a little while to herself with just the horse beneath her, the fresh breeze on her face . . . to look forward to seeing Simon again. And at the thought of him, the blood pulsed quicker through her veins and unconsciously she urged the mare forward and up the hill.

He was waiting in the shadow of the trees where she had first met him—a tall man on a tall, chestnut horse. The horses nickered softly to each other as she rode nearer. As she drew alongside, Simon reached out one hand, holding the reins with the other and she did the same. Their hands met and held, and Karen's face flushed with a glow of happiness, thrilling to the touch of the firm hand on hers.

"Good to see you again, Karen." The ordinary words of greeting covered a depth of feeling as Simon looked across into her face, his blue eyes dark with the emotion that was mirrored in Karen's hazel-coloured ones. She was surprised at the pulsing beat of her heart; the effect this man's touch could have on her.

After Keith, she had thought that no man could have the power to move her—not for a long time anyway, and yet here she was, the breath catching in her throat, feeling like a girl on her first date! She told herself that she was being a fool. Simon Asheby lived in a different world, didn't he? She was just someone who understood his love for his home and land, that was all, and she would be stupid to read more into his friendship than that!

It was cool and dim and beautiful inside Asheby Manor, just as Karen had imagined it would be. The gracious hall had a lovely sweeping double staircase leading round and upwards each side to a wide balcony from which many other doors opened. And Karen's eyes widened with delight at the sight of the intricately wrought balustrade and the glitter of the cut-glass chandelier overhead. The oak parquet floor shone with the years of loving polishing it had received in an age when time and care could be spent on it.

Simon took her riding hat and gloves, put them on a black marble-topped table and then, his hand cupping her elbow, he led her up a stairway to a room on the right.

Karen had a quick impression of loftiness—a tall room with a high, carved ceiling, of long windows with faded damask curtains, delicate Regency furniture, thick carpet and the smell of rose leaves.

Near the big Adam fireplace sat Simon's mother, her clothes expensively elegant.

She turned her head as they entered and Karen saw her likeness to her son—the same aristocratic nose, the firm mouth, the same air of good breeding.

"Mother, this is Nurse Karen Stevens, the young lady I told you about. She's working for John over at Coombe Magna . . ."

Lady Lillane Asheby extended a slender hand to Karen, her face wearing a smile so like her son's. Her skin was smooth and fine, her make-up perfectly applied and her voice was warm and welcoming.

"How do you do, my dear? I'm so pleased you could come. It's so good to have a new face around. Come and sit here where I can see you. Simon, ring for tea, will you?"

As she sat down, Karen watched the older woman's face with interest, and as she did so, she couldn't help but notice the thin bluish line round the lips, the faint breathlessness. Simon's mother had a heart disorder of some kind, Karen thought, with pity. No wonder he couldn't discuss his financial worries with her!

Lady Asheby was a charming person to talk to; interested in all Karen had to tell her about her work at St. Catherine's and now at Coombe Magna. Her questions were intelligent, her answers interesting, and the afternoon passed quickly as they all three sat there eating the thin sandwiches, the delicious cakes and drinking tea from the egg-shell china cups.

But gradually, as the conversation went on, Karen began to understand even more why Simon had so much worry, for his mother spoke as if they had an unlimited source of money to spend. Her ideas for the future; things she wanted to see and do and buy—told only too clearly of the need for a great wealth to back them up. Wealth that Simon and the impoverished estate could not possibly afford!

Karen could feel the tension growing in the tall, dark man seated beside her on the satin-striped Regency sofa. His mother's eyes sparkled, the thin line of blue round her lips deepening as she was telling Karen about a recent purchase.

"Fetch me the little package from my dressing table, darling, will you, please?" She turned blue eyes to her son, who rose at once to do her bidding.

When he came back his face was set

with barely concealed apprehension, and he handed over the small package saying—

"I hope you haven't been extravagant again, mother. You know I told you . . ."

"Simon—please! Not another lecture—not in front of Nurse Stevens!" The gentle voice was shocked, the blue eyes reproving, as she tore open the parcel with eager fingers.

"Look, my dear, isn't that just beautiful? I simply couldn't resist it. My jeweller in Harrogate kept it especially to show me."

She held out her hand to show Karen a thick, golden bracelet. It was indeed lovely; executed with all the skill and expertise of the goldsmith's art. It must have cost a small fortune, and Karen, whilst admiring and even coveting the bracelet, caught her breath. For Simon's face looked like a dark thunder-cloud! Forgotten was his resolution not to upset his mother; forgotten was the fact that they had a visitor.

"Mother—how could you? How could you buy that—that thing, when I've told you repeatedly how short of ready cash we are; how hard I'm struggling to keep our heads above water? You must take it back —at once!"

"Take it back!" his mother gasped. "Why should I, Simon? Don't be silly, son. I haven't had anything new for ages. Of course I won't take it back."

She dismissed the idea as preposterous, obviously thinking Simon was being tediously annoying—and in front of Karen, too!

At that, Simon's anger exploded, and he strode across the room and snatched the bracelet, box and all, from his mother's hands.

"Then *I* will, mother, and that's that! And I shall inform your jeweller friend that he's not to sell you any more baubles we cannot possibly afford!"

"Simon, how dare . . ." Rising from her seat, Lady Asheby began to gasp, and then clutched her chest with her blue-veined hands, her breathing suddenly more laboured, her blue eyes wide and frightened-looking.

Karen jumped up quickly, calling to Simon—

"Quick, get your mother's tablets,

capsules or whatever she's prescribed, Simon . . ." and she bent over the stricken woman, easing her gently into a heap of cushions. "Take it easy, Lady Asheby, gently now . . ."

She loosened the older woman's clothing, and as Simon came back again, she crushed the small glass capsule and broke it open and held it beneath Lady Asheby's nose, so that she could inhale the vapour. Gradually, slowly, the laboured breathing eased; the bluish tinge faded a little; the pinched nose lost a little of its pallor. Simon, after throwing the long windows even wider open, had stood helplessly watching, despair and remorse written clearly on his handsome face; two deep lines etched more deeply each side of his mouth.

"Stay—stay with me, nurse." The words were thin and low.

"Don't worry, Lady Asheby, you're doing fine now. Just rest there quietly. Here, let me give you another cushion. That better?" Karen's quiet composure evidently calmed the frightened woman, for she managed a wavering smile of gratitude.

"Ring for your mother's doctor, will you, Simon? I'll stay with her; don't worry, she's recovering now . . ."

As Simon left the room, Karen's pitying glance followed him; what an awful position to be in! His mother obviously suffered from angina pectoris, and he would feel guilty every time he upset her. And yet he had to make her understand that her husband's wealth had long since been swallowed up; that her son was having such difficulty in hanging on to their estate.

In the gathering dusk, Karen talked gently and softly, reassuring Lady Asheby and Simon as they waited for the doctor to arrive.

"He said he would finish evening surgery first, Karen, when I told him you were here, and that mother had recovered somewhat."

Indeed, his mother's pulse rate had steadied and her breathing eased, and Karen had time to worry about missing Dr. Henshaw's surgery at Coombe Magna. Although she was sure Mrs. Roberts could cope, she wished this had not happened on this particular night!

After the Ashebys' doctor had been and gone, Karen saw the patient tucked up quietly in bed and in the care of an elderly maid, and Simon offered to run her back to Coombe Magna in his car.

"It's getting dark outside, Karen. Too dark for you to ride Brown Belle back. Leave her here—I'll see she's returned in the morning. Come on, I'll have you back at Coombe Magna in a few minutes."

But all the same, it was quite late when Karen got out of his car at the entrance to the Medical Unit.

"Bless you, Karen," Simon gave her hand a quick affectionate squeeze of gratitude. "Goodnight, my dear . . ."

The lights were still on in the building and she hurried inside, hoping Mrs. Roberts had managed all right.

"Where the devil have you been, Karen? Or need I ask, seeing that you just arrived back in Simon Asheby's car?"

Karen's face paled at this reception. Dr. Matthew Henshaw's face was as black as thunder, his voice hard and accusing . . . The sound of anger in his voice pulled Karen up with a jerk. She dropped her riding hat and gloves on the table and looked round.

"Where's Mrs. Roberts?" she asked.

"I had to let her go. Apparently, as you said you would be back, she arranged to test some of her junior St. John's cadets tonight, and rather than let her down, I said I would manage here until you came. Of course, I didn't expect you to make an evening of your gallivanting about, Karen." The sarcasm in his voice made Karen's anger flare up.

"I'm sorry, Dr. Henshaw, to be back so late. Unfortunately, Simon's mother was taken ill. She has angina and I couldn't leave her immediately. Naturally, I thought Mrs. Roberts would stay on to look after your surgery session. I'm sorry."

Her brown eyes were flecked with amber lights and her chin stuck out defiantly and she looked anything but penitent. With her soft cheeks flushed, her hair dishevelled, she nevertheless looked very pretty right then.

"I should have thought the wealthy Hon Simon could afford a full-time nurse for his sick mother!" Matthew Henshaw's voice had a sarcastic bitterness that shocked Karen.

Was the doctor jealous? Why on earth was he so antagonistic towards Simon Asheby, she thought, and longed to explain that, far from being wealthy, the Ashebys had a difficult struggle to keep going. But she had promised Simon not to reveal what he had told her, so she compressed her lips and said nothing, but her eyes told the watching man that she would have dearly loved to lash out in reply!

"Was there anything special tonight, doctor?" she asked coldly, and when he replied that there had been nothing that he couldn't cope with by himself, she almost sniffed in disgust! And then, remembering her St. Catherine's training where matron had insisted that all nurses, senior and junior, treated all the doctors, young or old, with the utmost respect, she refrained, but that give-away face of hers must have told its own tale, for suddenly Matthew Henshaw gave a wry smile.

"Sparks always seem to fly whenever you and I get together, don't they, Karen? I'm sorry, I shouldn't have blown up about your being late. You were quite right to stay with Lady Asheby if you considered she needed you there. I'm sure you're too good a nurse not to consider your patient first."

"I did." The two words fell flatly between them, for Karen refused to be mollified by his apology, and the doctor watched her face ruefully and then sighed.

"Ah well. Now then, what about these other troubles Lisa told me about?"

"Troubles? Look, Dr. Henshaw, I know I'm new here and Lisa Felstead's not, but she's far from co-operative! She goes out of her way to be difficult and unhelpful. For instance, I need some sort of understanding with your local hospital about admitting emergencies at once. Must I contact you first, or can I get your confirmation later—perhaps too late? Miss Felstead told you I'd asked about that, did she?"

And from the slow flush that stained his rugged cheeks, Karen knew her instinct had been right. Lisa Felstead had not mentioned the matter to him at all!

"Did she tell you about those two cases of food poisoning we've had, doctor? Or the test we need of the water from the pool?"

Karen saw Matthew swallow hard, and she knew once more that she was right. Lisa Felstead was deliberately trying to create trouble for her.

"Mrs. Roberts told me about the Parker-Smiths and I've been in to see them. They're doing fine, Karen. I'll get your water test done for you and see that it's done regularly. The pool's a fairly new thing and the council officers are a bit lax here—so much else to do in the high season, I suppose."

Just then a young mother brought in her little boy who was sobbing bitterly. He had run away, trying to escape his bedtime, and had fallen down and badly grazed his knee. Since then, he had stubbornly refused to let his mother treat it. It was long past his bedtime now, and the knee was hurting him.

"Suppose you choose a sweetie, Jason, out of my special tin? They're only for badly wounded soldiers and brave little boys."

The child's sobs ceased as he looked up at her, his round eyes wide with interest.

"You'll have to have an enormous bandage on that knee, Jason," Karen added, knowing from past experience that small boys just loved showing off a dressing. No doubt young Jason would go about with a well-affected limp—for a few minutes—or until he forgot and went racing on!

There were more tears as Karen gently cleansed and dressed the small, dimpled knee; finally applying a huge bandage lightly fixed, to make much of the injury. As she finished, she was amused to see Jason surveying the result with proud satisfaction.

"Off you go, wounded soldier, and come back in the morning, eh?"

As she cleared away the basin and the soiled swabs, she caught sight of Matthew Henshaw's face. It held an almost tender look and he smiled, saying softly—

"You'll do, young Karen, you'll do . . ." and to her utter disgust, the words brought a flush of pleasure and embarrassment to her cheeks. Words of praise from Matthew Henshaw—oh, Karen was truly annoyed with herself for the glow of warmth they gave her. Her startled eyes were raised to his and for a moment the air was electric with the tension between them.

"I'm sorry about Lisa's awkwardness, Karen. I—I think she's jealous of you," he said disconcertingly.

"Jealous of me?" Karen's heart lurched.

"Sit down, Karen. I'll make us a cup of coffee. Where do you keep the things?" And to her surprise, he did so quite efficiently. He brought it through, saying—

"Let me tell you about Lisa Felstead, Karen . . ." he began, and there, with the rest of Coombe Magna beginning to enjoy the evening's entertainment all around them; there in the quietness of the Medical Unit, he told her of how Lisa's father, Professor Felstead, had helped him to become a doctor. "After my own father died, he encouraged me to finish my training; helped and advised me in every way. Lisa and I were thrown together, and because of my obligations to her father, I suppose, I keep her as my secretary. A very good one she is, too, that is—except when she comes up against another pretty girl, and then her jealousy shows. Oh, I know it makes me sound sort of . . ." he shrugged, struggling for the right words. "But she wants to be first in my life, to be important to my career, as her father was. Funny thing is, she doesn't really need to work; her folks are quite comfortably off, so I appreciate that, too."

As he told her all this, Karen could well imagine how it was with him; his gratitude and appreciation for what the Felsteads had done for him. But did he know that Lisa was in love with him? Did he know that old devil propinquity would see that Lisa would stay in love with him while she worked so closely with him? He must know—or be completely blind, and did he love Lisa?

Somehow that last question made Karen's heart ache with a peculiar tightness in her breast that she found puzzling. He must love Lisa; she was so lovely to look at, and I bet she's not so cold and aloof with him, she thought wryly.

"Give her time, Karen, and I'm sure you two will become friends," he finished, and not for the first time Karen wondered at the blindness of the male of the species, for she knew quite well that Lisa, in love with Matthew, would never be her friend.

After he had left, she rang Asheby Manor to ask Simon how his mother was.

"She seems all right now, Karen. Thank you for your help. I'm so sorry you were involved in a family scene, my dear." And Karen could sense from his tone just how much he disliked her knowing what had happened that afternoon. After all, she was an outsider, and he was a proud man.

"I can be discreet, Simon, please forget it—I shall," she answered quietly.

"The bracelet goes back to the jeweller tomorrow," he told her, "and as soon as my mother is fitter, I'll try again to make her understand how things really are. Trouble is," he added with a faint laugh, "my father always spoiled her terribly."

A few seconds later she rang off, her heart full of sympathy for Simon; understanding his pride and love for Asheby, yet hating to be harsh with his mother. It wasn't always easy for the upper classes, she reflected as she changed out of uniform into a pretty dress.

On her way across to the ballroom, she

saw Mavis, the girl in charge of the flower arrangements, and had an idea.

"Oh, Mavis, be a love and do something for me, will you?"

The other girl smiled showing two beautiful dimples.

"It's all according to what you want, Karen."

"I'd like to send some flowers up to Asheby Manor for Lady Asheby. I met her today and she's not very well just now." Karen bit her lip, and then went on, "Trouble is, Mavis, she's got plenty of gorgeous blooms in the grounds and glass-houses . . ."

"No problem, pet. Let me make up a special little basket arrangement of simple flowers—the nice-smelling ones, nothing grand. She'll probably appreciate them all the more."

"What a good idea, bless you," Karen thanked the other girl warmly. "Let me have the bill, won't you?"

"Will do. I'll put in a little card with your best wishes, shall I?"

Pleased with this arrangement, Karen hurried on to the ballroom. As usual, there was dancing there that evening with Pete introducing the numbers as well as singing some of the latest pop songs in a pleasant, trendy voice. At other times, Penny joined him in duet numbers while in between she organised spot prize dances, gyrating energetically on the polished floor, getting wallflowers together, and generally seeing that everyone had a good time.

Karen noticed that the glamorous Angela, looking especially lovely in a dress of iridescent blue-green, made a constant beeline for Pete. He had to be friendly with everyone; it was part of his job, but *she* took this to be a personal compliment, and once or twice Penny's lips tightened at the sight of Angela clinging closely, tightly, to her husband as they danced.

Karen also noticed that young Joanne Thorpe hadn't danced once all the evening. Instead, she sat, her eyes wistfully watching the others, beside a grim-faced, grey haired man Karen took to be her father.

Drawing a deep breath, Karen circled the floor—it was now or never! As she passed Pete, she murmured—

"Do me a favour, Pete—ask that girl

over there to dance. I want a chance to speak to her father."

"Sure thing, Karen," and a few moments later, he had persuaded a rather reluctant Joanne to join him and the others on the floor in a lively number.

"It's Joanne's father, isn't it?" Quickly, before she lost her nerve, Karen introduced herself. With a brief nod, he resumed his seat, his face turned away as if to discourage any further conversation, but she wasn't going to be put off as easily as that!

"She's a lovely girl, Joanne, Mr. Thorpe —you must be proud of her. Pity though that she's so shy. I expect you wish she'd join in more with the youngsters here?"

"Join in?" he almost barked, his brows rising, his lips pinched; his face so fiercely angry that Karen understood why Joanne was so afraid of him. "She's no need to 'join in' as you call it, Miss Stevens, she has me and quite enough to do looking after me. I'm a busy man—I've no time to waste . . ." he paused looking round the ballroom with evident distaste. "I'm only here tonight because Joanne went on and on. And now I'm going . . ."

As he made to rise, Karen clutched his arm tightly; anger, white-hot anger, blazing in her brown eyes at this man's incredible selfishness!

"But she's only young—she deserves some fun, some life of her own, with young people of her own age. You must see that, Mr. Thorpe." She swallowed hard and then went on more softly, "You'll lose her altogether, you know. Lose her and her affection, because she'll grow to hate you—as all prisoners hate their jailers!"

"How dare you talk to me like this," he spluttered. "I'll . . ."

"Please—oh, please—I'm only doing this for Joanne's sake. And yours, too, if you weren't too blind to see it!"

Without giving him time to reply; holding tightly to his arm so that he could not leave without making a little scene, Karen talked rapidly, heatedly, pouring out all her genuine concern at Joanne's unhappiness.

Pete, seeing her so engrossed, took Joanne on to the floor for another dance. And gradually, Karen could sense some softening, some relenting in the thin-faced man beside her. Quick to press home her advantage, she added—

"Joanne tells me she likes to swim, but is rather put off by all the crowd round the bathing pool here. I wonder, please, Mr. Thorpe, if you would let her take lessons—down in the private little bay, in underwater snorkelling, that sort of thing? Please?"

The man looked across intently into her beseeching eyes, and then slowly nodded.

"Well, yes," he agreed grudgingly. "Yes, well, I'll see. Perhaps you're right, Miss Stevens, Joanne does need to spread her wings a little. But I want none of that for her . . ." and he gave a firm nod in the direction of Angela, who, surrounded as usual by a rather boisterous crowd, was laughing and talking too loudly.

Karen agreed. "I'll keep an eye on Joanne, don't worry. And thank you for listening to me, Mr. Thorpe."

He gave a twisted sort of smile that looked out of place on his stern face.

"Thank *you*, Miss Stevens. I'm sure you mean well . . ." and with that he rose, bidding her a curt goodnight, and left the ballroom.

A few seconds later, a breathless Joanne flopped into the vacated chair.

"Oh, Karen, I saw you talking to Dad." Her blue eyes were filled with anxiety. "What did you—he say?"

Karen, still glowing with mild triumph, patted her hand and smiled.

"It's all right, you can have your lessons, Joanne . . ."

Much later, Karen's legs were getting tired. She had danced every dance from then on, helping Penny to encourage and partner the shyest, awkwardest of guests. She felt she owed this to Mr. John, who had just made a brief appearance, looking large and hearty and thoroughly out of place on the dance floor, and then had beaten a hasty retreat to play billiards with others of the same mind, away from the music and the noise of the ballroom.

Leaving a note for Sandy, the young beach instructor, in his pigeon-hole about lessons for Joanne Thorpe, she went wearily across to her own little bedroom. What a day. . . !

6

THE next morning saw the usual crop of casualties, amongst them her young friend, Ricky Williams. He sat patiently waiting his turn, stoically, and then held up his grubby hand as he came through to the surgery.

"Look, nurse—my best hook, too," and Karen saw that he had a fish hook in his finger.

"I thought the idea was to hook the fish, not your hand, Ricky? I've heard of fish fingers, but this is ridiculous," she joked.

Ricky raised his eyes heavenwards at the feeble pun, and then set his lips tightly as Karen, after disinfecting the shaft of the hook, pulled it through as quickly and as gently as she could so that she was able to cut off the barbed end. Thoroughly cleansing the wound, she told Ricky to keep the dressing clean, knowing, of course, that he wouldn't!

"Okay, Ricky, love. Help yourself to a sweet—no, take two. One for losing your best hook. Sorry I had to cut it—couldn't pull it back out again, you know."

"Couldn't have gone fishing . . ." he muttered to himself. "Should have gone down to the beach with Penny to do the sand castle competition but I heard her and Pete having a row this morning; thought she'd be in a bit of a huff, so I went fishing instead . . ."

As he chattered on, Karen wondered what had caused the Naylors to quarrel; they were usually so happy together. Trust young Ricky to overhear it, too; he missed nothing, did he?

Just as he was leaving, a middle-aged man, his face anxious and worried-looking, came into the waiting room.

"Oh, nurse, I wonder if you'd have a look at my wife?"

"Of course. Can you tell me what's the matter?"

"Pains in the stomach or something. Been awake all night, she has. Shall I ring for the doctor?" He ran his hand distractedly through his thinning hair, and Karen felt sorry for him, for things seem worse when you're away from home and on holiday.

"I'll see her first, Mr—er—Walters, and then I'll get the doctor if necessary. Please don't worry, I'll come at once."

Leaving a note as usual, Karen locked the door and hurried across to the Walters' bungalow, where she found Mrs. Walters writhing in pain on her bed.

"Oh, nurse, I'm so glad you've come— I've been in awful pain all night and nothing seems to ease it. I've tried a warm bottle on my stomach, but the pain still keeps coming and going badly . . ."

Even as she spoke, she tightened up with another spasm of pain, and when it had passed somewhat, Karen rolled up her nightie gently probing with firm, warm fingers.

"Could it be my appendix, nurse? It is down there, isn't it?"

"Have you been sick, Mrs. Walters?" Karen asked.

"No, but I feel as if I might be at any moment. The pain starts here, but mostly finishes here, and—oh . . ."

Karen watched as the woman cringed and then tightened against another spasm of pain. When it had passed, she pressed firmly on one small area under Mrs.

Walters' right ribs, and saw her wince deeply.

"I'll get Dr. Henshaw to come in at once, Mrs. Walters, don't worry, you'll be all right till then," she soothed and secretly hoped she was right! What was the old saying about "fair, fat and forty". Well, Mrs. Walters was all of those. Yes, it well could be . . .

She rang the doctors' surgery as soon as she got back to the Medical Unit. This time, she firmly refused to be sidetracked by the obstinate Miss Felstead!

"Put me on to Dr. Henshaw—at once, please."

"He's busy, nurse, he has a patient with him right now."

"Please do as I ask, this could well be an emergency," Karen snapped, but it was a few minutes before she heard the doctor's terse—

"Yes, nurse, what is it now?"

Karen wasn't to know that Lisa had passed on her message with the suggestion that the nurse from Coombe Magna was probably in a panic about nothing, as usual . . . Lisa Felstead was clever; her insinuations were subtle, often taking the

159

doctor in completely. But this time she was wrong although Matthew was not to know that then, as he answered Karen.

"I have a patient, a Mrs. Walters, doctor, who's in considerable abdominal pain. It could be appendicitis, but . . ." she paused.

"But what, nurse?" The voice at the other end sounded irritable. He had been up for most of the night with an emergency, and his waiting room was overflowing with his own patients and those of one of the other doctor who was off duty.

"I think it's inflammation of the gall bladder, doctor."

"Leave the diagnosis to me, nurse," he snapped. "I'll come at once."

Well, of all the . . . ! His words hurt her. Gone was the feeling of closer understanding they had reached the night before. She felt he was making her inferior status very clear; it was not the job of the nurse to offer a doctor a diagnosis.

She watched for his car, and when he arrived, looking rather wan and tired, she took him immediately across to the Walters' bungalow. Quickly, without preamble, he examined the patient, whose pains had now eased a little, but she still gasped aloud as his searching fingers found the seat of the pain. He asked a few pertinent questions, a frown between his brows, and then said,

"It's not your appendix, Mrs. Walters, you've a gall bladder inflammation here. I'll give you some tablets to get rid of that first, and then you'll have to have some tests and X-rays to see if you have gallstones. The tablets should relieve the pain within the next four days. Keep off fatty foods meanwhile and take it easy."

He patted her shoulder, and the look of relief on her face was obvious.

"Thank you, doctor. You, too, nurse."

As they walked back to the Medical Unit, Karen suggested a cup of coffee.

"I've a waiting room full of patients needing my attention, Karen."

"I'm sorry, Dr. Henshaw. At least Mrs. Walters wasn't so bad as I first suspected." Karen hoped he might mention her correct diagnosis, but he didn't. His face wore a sombre look and she wondered what on earth had upset him. That he was tired, that one of his more gossipy patients had mentioned seeing her riding with Simon

Asheby the afternoon before to Lisa Felstead who had lost no time in passing the bit of news on to him—all this she wasn't to know, so as they walked side by side along the path towards the Medical Unit, she said casually—

"Lady Asheby's much better, too, I'm told, so . . ."

"And you're concerned about *her*, aren't you, Karen," he interrupted savagely. "After all, you're hoping she might be your future mother-in-law, I suppose?"

"Well, of all the. . . ! Of course not, I . . ." Karen stammered, completely taken off guard.

"Well, let me tell you, my girl, I've no time for nurses who only use their job as a stop-gap until marriage." His voice was raw and for one wild, fleeting moment, she could have sworn that he was—well, jealous? No—never, she must be wrong, but he certainly sounded upset and angry about something, that was for sure!

She felt childishly near to tears. She had half expected praise, not this tirade, and after their more friendly closeness last night, this morning's coolness hit her hard!

162

Then her temper began to rise; he was utterly impossible in his childish dislike of the Ashebys. As for her trying to marry into the family, why—that was crazy!

"Dr. Henshaw," she stormed indignantly, "I *like* my job. It comes before any thought of catching a husband, I can assure you. I try to be a good nurse before all else, and I don't know what makes you think . . ." she paused for breath, and then at the sight of the look on his face, she exploded, "As for you—why if Florence Nightingale had ever worked with you, she'd have blown out her lamp, I reckon!"

And with that she flounced into the inner surgery, leaving him standing there. She heard the outer door slam, and a moment later, the roar of his car engine. For the rest of the morning, she seethed inwardly, mostly with anger, but partly with regret that they could never be, well —good working partners, if not friends.

Strolling back casually after lunch, she ran into young Joanne, a bundle of towels under her arm, her face alight with anticipation.

"It worked, Karen," she began

excitedly. "I'm just off for my first lesson. Bit early actually, but I'm rather scared. Anyway, it was something that my father finally agreed, wasn't it?"

"I'm sure you'll be all right; I've heard that young Sandy is very good at his job —dishy, too," Karen teased, and was surprised to see a soft flush of colour creep into the other girl's cheeks.

A few steps further along, Joanne began hesitatingly—

"I wish I could do something with my hair, Karen. It's so—so ordinary . . ."

Karen took a swift look at the young girl's face and saw that she was serious.

"I think your hair's great, Joanne—it would be such a shame to cut it short. Perhaps a little off wouldn't hurt," she paused, considering. "I know—why don't you have it high-lighted? You know, get a few light streaks put in professionally. Felice here, is very good, they say."

"Highlights? Oh, I don't know," Joanne was dubious. "Besides, what would Dad say? And I daren't have Felice come over to our place."

"He probably wouldn't even notice. Anyway, if he did, just tell him it's the sea air and the sun down here that's lightened it."

"What a fib!" The younger girl giggled, and Karen joined in.

"I know, but what your father doesn't know about, won't hurt him, I reckon! Anyway, you can come to my place and have Felice do you there, using my bathroom and so on."

After a few moments reflection, kicking the pebbles with the toe of her sandal, Joanne turned to Karen.

"I'll do that. Thanks, Karen."

"Come on then, before you change your mind. I want to see Felice anyway."

Five minutes later, the appointment fixed, Joanne slipped off for her first underwater session on the beach, leaving the nurse and hairdresser sipping yet another mug of coffee.

"How's the rash, Felice?"

"M'mm? Oh, you were right, Karen, it was those cheap rubber gloves—or something on the lining of them. I'm back to my old brand, and the rash is better now. I'm using the doctor's cream though when I can."

At the mention of the doctor, a shadow

fell across Karen's face as she remembered the scene that morning; it was almost time to get back to the Medical Unit.

As she hurried back, she passed young Ricky's pal . . . what was his name? Ah yes, Luke, and somehow she couldn't repress a shudder. Something about that boy gave her the creeps; he looked so sly, with an almost-adult evil look about him, especially right then, as he passed her, intent on mischief.

Then Karen recalled young Ricky's remarks about Penny and Pete quarelling, and kept her eyes open for them as she went about her work . . .

During the next few days, she noticed that Penny's face didn't look so happy and bright as usual. In fact, Karen could have sworn that she had been crying once or twice, but as the other girl wore clever eye make-up, it was hard to tell especially from a distance. When Penny was organising the second heats of the tennis competition, Pete was doing the same for the swimmers at the pool. And outstandingly successful amongst his contestants was Angela Manning, who was making a shameless bid for his attention!

Karen knew that as part of his job he had to make himself charming to everyone, but wasn't he overdoing it a bit when it came to the curvaceous Angela? It was hard to tell; all the girls flocked around him, and he laughed and teased them all. Karen hoped for Penny's sake that he was only being polite and friendly to Angela as part of his job! Pity *that* young woman hadn't anything better to do.

Her mother was a different person now that she could hold queenly court with her bridge-playing friends. With a daily heat and massage treatment, and something at last to take her mind off herself and her pain, she was looking much better. Like all good nurses, Karen realised that drugs and surgery could do only so much—the rest is up to the patient! Well, she had achieved something with Mrs. Manning, and she knew John Lyle-Coombe was pleased with her results.

"Why don't you go for a breath of fresh air, Nurse Stevens, while I get cleaned up in here?—do you good." The cleaning lady was fast becoming another of Karen's friends.

"It's not my off-duty time though . . ." Karen replied doubtfully, but with a touch of longing in her voice. "But I would like to go down to the bay; I've not seen it yet. I suppose if anything serious came up, you could send someone for me? I'll only be a little while, and there's hardly anyone around yet, is there?"

The older woman's face creased into a sunny smile.

"Oh, go on, nurse, get going. I'll keep an eye open here . . ."

And that's how Karen came to be walking slowly across the beach, almost deserted as yet; scuffing the fine sand between the toes of her sandals. The early morning sea was calm—a sparkling, clear blue with white lace edges to the rippling little waves lapping the fine yellow sand. It was a lovely, peaceful morning, and Karen lifted her face to the sun, already shedding its warmth. The sky overhead was clear, with only one or two cotton-wool puffs of cloud, depicting another gloriously fine day. She filled her lungs with fresh sea air on a deep sigh of contentment; this is the life, she thought blissfully.

That bliss was all too soon to be shattered . . . Firstly, by the sight of a figure scurrying along the cliff top. Even from the distance, Karen recognised the chubby, solid figure of young Luke Martin, and something in his manner made her apprehensive. What was he up to now? she wondered, sorry the moment of peace had been disturbed.

Then suddenly she heard voices behind her, calling—

"Miss! Oh, miss, look! Hurry, please come and see. Up there!"

A group of small children, local youngsters by their accent, their faces scared-looking and apprehensive, were suddenly crowding round her, pulling at her dress, tugging at her hands.

"What? Er—what's the matter?" She looked round and then her startled glance followed their pointing fingers.

"Look—up there!"

For a moment the rays of the early sun blinded her eyes, and then she saw it; what appeared to be a bundle of rags. A limp bundle, sprawled on a tiny ledge half way up the cliff edge; the jagged, rugged, red cliff face that overlooked the small bay.

"It's a boy, an' he's dead, miss!" jabbered one child excitedly.

"Sure to be, miss, if he fell down from up there," agreed another, relishing the drama.

By then Karen's eyes had adjusted themselves and her heart began to hammer uncontrollably. Didn't she recognise that tattered pair of brief shorts—that tee shirt with the black lettering on it? Oh no— not Ricky! Not that lovable, gap-toothed bundle of mischief who was her first and dearest friend at Coombe Magna—not Ricky! Karen caught her breath on a half sob and began to run to the foot of the cliff.

He was so still, sprawled there like a lifeless doll. Even as the thought crossed her mind, she was glad that he wasn't conscious; if he moved he would fall. Fall to be brutally hurt, or killed, by the rocks below.

The escarpment was not really high, not as cliff faces go, but to Karen climbing, inching her way upwards, it seemed to go on and up for ever.

"Don't look down, Karen my girl, don't look down" she told herself fiercely, knowing how desperately afraid of heights she was! Remembering ruefully that usually a six-foot ladder made her ears pop!

Her breath came in short, painful gasps and she wished she had something more substantial on her feet than her flimsy sandals. It seemed an age—a year-long age —before she reached the limp body. It *was* Ricky; his face was ghastly white with the cuts and bruises showing already dark upon it.

There was barely enough room for Karen to squeeze herself beside him on the narrow ledge. Clutching the rock face with the desperately seeking fingers of one hand, she carefully explored the young body for breakages with the other, and to her heartfelt relief, she didn't find any. Thank God, he hadn't broken anything in his fall, although a blow on the head had rendered him unconscious.

Once she had established this, she was able to ease him, inch by careful inch, a little more upright, giving herself a few more feet to crouch alongside him. It was only after she had managed this that she realised that somehow she had to get him up—or down!

The group of interested spectators down below seemed to be stunned into immobility as they craned their necks up to watch her, and she was far too afraid to look down at them. Surely someone would have had the sense to send for help, even though it would take a little while to get round to the road?

The sun was gradually getting higher, and the heat beat down on her head until the haze made her feel sick and giddy now that the first shock had passed . . . now that she could no longer move. Gradually, too, pins and needles played havoc in her cramped limbs.

Then suddenly, above the noise below, the cries of the seagulls high above her in the sky, the soft distant lap of the waves, she heard something else—the sharp, clear warning bark of a dog—and it came from above. Gently she forced back her head, pressing her chin away from the hard rock as far as she dare. Never before had an angel from heaven appeared in the shape of a fat old corgi—Matthew Henshaw's dog!

"Help . . . down here! Please—down here, help me . . ." she yelled in a hoarse voice.

Dust and rock pebbles began to slither down, and then she saw a man's face and shoulders appear over the edge above.

"Matthew—oh, help me please! It's young Ricky—he's hurt."

"Hold on," he called. "How much room have you got, Karen?"

"None, and I can't move, up or down. Ricky's unconscious . . ."

More pebbles cascaded down as Matthew Henshaw inched his head and shoulders further over the edge above.

"I'll have to get help—a rope or something. Can you hold on?" he called again, the words almost carried away on the breeze.

"Yes, but please hurry—I'm scared," she answered in a voice that wobbled with fear.

Ages passed, and Ricky stirred once, long lashes fluttering, and Karen clutched him tightly, afraid that any sudden movement he might make would send them both plummeting downwards. The heat began to prickle her skin; insects buzzed in her ears, and time passed on leaden feet as she clung there, her legs growing numb as she grew more and more afraid that she might let go!

At last, something snaked its way downwards from above her head, a sort of cradle made of rope.

"Pass the lowest strand under his backside, Karen, if you can. Call out when you want us to start pulling up. Guide his body as we lever it up; it's a bit smoother further up . . ."

Somehow, they got the swinging bundle aloft, leaving Karen strangely alone; standing there with her body pressed hard to the rock face, her knees weak and without any strength of their own, her hands clammy with sweat.

"Now you, Karen . . ." someone called, and she shuddered.

"I—I can't. I daren't leave go. It's no use, Matthew, I daren't move . . ." her voice broke on a sob.

She heard the discussion going on; moved her head slightly to avoid a fresh fall of stones; shivering now with shock and fright.

Then she heard it—a stern, deep voice, resounding firmly—

"Nurse Stevens, pull yourself together. You're needed up here, so get started . . ."

Rousing her as nothing else could have done, the doctor's angry voice set her numbed limbs into motion, and a few minutes later, willing hands reached out to hoist her on to firm ground at the top. Her legs were unable to support her, and she would have crumpled into a heap on the coarse grass if Matthew Henshaw had not held her close.

A sense of security, a wonderful sense of comfort passed over her as she stayed there held close by his strong arms. To Karen it felt the most wonderful place in the world to be right then—this pair of arms.

"You shortened my life by about ten years, young Karen! Feel alright? Sorry I had to blast away at you, but it was the only thing I could think of," he said, his breath warm against her chestnut hair. "Thank God I was walking the dog . . ."

She gave him a wavering smile, and brushed the dirt from the cheek that, a few minutes before, had been pressed tightly against the gritty-surfaced rock below.

"How's young Ricky?"

"Safe by now in the tender care of our Mrs. Roberts, I reckon," the doctor replied. "Now, come on, it's a good old soak in the bath for you, my girl, and a cup of sweet tea."

Word had spread quickly round the Coombe Magna complex, and Karen found herself the heroine of the hour when she finally emerged for her meal that night. She had decided to keep young Ricky tucked up in one of the cubicles for the night—under observation, she told his distracted mother. His superficial injuries had been attended to, but he seemed lethargic and tired, quite subdued and unlike his usual active self.

When he was still rather drowsy the next morning, Karen decided that she would seek a second opinion, so she rang the doctor's surgery. He arrived later that morning, and Karen's face flushed as he came through the door; the memory of the previous morning clearly in her thoughts.

But to her dismay, however, he was followed in by Lisa Felstead . . .

"Lisa's coming with me on my rounds this morning, nurse, she rarely gets to see the outlying districts," he explained casually.

Actually, he was hoping to get the two girls together more; to try and see if they couldn't become more friendly towards each other. Manlike, he was oblivious to the strained atmosphere right then!

"I wanted to see you about young Ricky, doctor," Karen said, her clear eyes suddenly veiled, her manner professional to a degree! She went on to tell him of her suspicions and then followed him through to the little cubicle.

"How's our Sherpa friend this morning, then?" He ruffled Ricky's hair, but the youngster only winced and gave a weak imitation of his usual sunny smile. "Let's have a look at you, Ricky." Chatting soothingly all the time, the doctor examined the patient and then when they returned to the surgery, he said—

"I believe you're right, Karen. We'll have him down to the General Hospital for an X-ray, shall we? Clever girl to spot it —it's quite easily overlooked."

At the warmth of his approval, Karen saw a shadow pass over Lisa Felstead's smooth face.

"I'll let his mother know at once, doctor. Thank you," Karen smiled radiantly; for once she had done something right—and in front of the snooty, raven-haired Miss Felstead, too!

"How's the inflamed gall-bladder, Karen?"

"Much better; the tablets have worked well, and I think she'll do until she gets home . . ." Chatting about one or two other cases for a while, Karen felt more at ease than she had in the doctor's presence for a long time, but Lisa looked pointedly at her watch, reminding him of other calls he had to make.

And later that morning, Karen kept thinking of the two of them together in his car, out in the lovely countryside; perhaps stopping for lunch at some nice little inn. And she wondered just why the picture bothered her so much; why the heavy ache inside her?

Ricky seemed a little brighter after a

light lunch, and Karen hoped she was doing right when she asked him gently—

"How did you come to fall down the cliff, pet?"

A closed-in, stubborn look crossed the young face; his fingers nervously pleated the edge of the sheet, his eyes refusing to meet hers. Suddenly, a picture flashed across Karen's mind's eye—that of the figure she had seen a few moments before they had discovered the fallen boy. Luke Martin!

"Did Luke have anything to do with it, Ricky? Come on, pet, you can tell me—you do know I don't sneak . . ." She reached out and covered the fidgeting hand with her own, and he burst out—

"It was the nest—gull's eggs they were. He was going to take them—just over the edge—he told me so. I told him to leave them alone, but he only laughed and pushed me away." He swallowed convulsively, his voice low. "We sort of struggled, but he's bigger than me, and he pushed me hard. Oh, Karen," he buried his head in his arms, "it was awful—I felt all the sharp edges, then suddenly it sort of went black . . ."

"Shush, never mind, pet. You're alright now—just a bad bump on the head, that's all."

All the same, she meant to have words with Master Luke—the next time she saw him.

But she didn't have so long to wait for, to her intense surprise, when she answered a tentative knock on her office door, she found the very person she was wanting to see, standing there!

"It's me, nurse. I've come to see Ricky. Can I, please? And I've brought these for him." "These" were an armful of goodies for the patient—sweets, comics, games and so on.

"No, Luke, I'm afraid you can't see Ricky just now." Firmly, she took the boy's arm and steered him out into the empty waiting-room.

"Sit down, Luke, I want a chat with you." The sullen-faced youngster looked up warily, his eyes shifting to measure the distance between her and the door, and reading his mind, Karen said—

"Oh, no you don't, my lad, you'll stay here until I've finished with you. '

"I'll tell my Mum about you . . ." he threatened, squirming on the seat.

"Perhaps I'll have something to tell her, too, Luke. Like how you tried to kill your little mate, Ricky!" Karen deliberately filled the words with all the drama she could muster; to her way of thinking, this young monster needed to be taught a lesson.

"Kill him!" he gasped. "No, I didn't . . ."

"Then how did he come to fall over the cliff?"

"We were fighting—and he sort of fell . . ." the other's composure began to crumple.

"You pushed him! In any case, you're much bigger and heavier than he is. You're jolly lucky, my boy, that you're not in prison right now for manslaughter or something." Karen had made a good job of the scare! Two big, shiny tears glistened down the fat cheeks, and he sniffed loudly.

"Go on, stick up for him. Everybody likes him, an' not me," his shoulders slumped, his voice full of self-pity.

"There's not much to like about a boy who wants to steal birds' eggs, and then almost kills his best mate," Karen shook her head emphatically, "No, I guess there's not much to like about you."

At that, the boy began crying loudly, the words tumbling out between the muffled sobs.

"Will Ricky get better, miss? I won't ever try to pinch the birds' eggs again, honest!"

Somehow, he looked so pathetic slumped there, that Karen's soft heart relented and she scolded herself for being so harsh. She patted his shoulders, her voice softer.

"He'll be all right, Luke, so let's hear no more about it. I won't tell your mother, or anyone else, but you'd better watch your step, my lad, from now on. Okay, off you go—leave these here and I'll see that Ricky gets them as soon as he's well enough."

She rose, looking down at the boy; wondering just how much love and care he had ever known from his famous mother and her string of short-while husbands? Poor kid, what chance had he had?

Suddenly, with a strangled gasp, Luke

reached up and clutched round her legs, burying his blotchy face in her skirt.

"I wish you were my mate—like you are Ricky's . . ." and without thinking, Karen held the unhappy boy closer, patting his heaving shoulders, her heart full of pity.

"Behave yourself and I could well be just that, pet, before you go . . ."

Just then the phone on her desk rang, and she ushered the boy out. It was Simon to ask if she would be riding over his way that afternoon?

"No chance, Simon, I'm more or less on duty all day today. Actually, I ache all over . . ." and she told him of the adventure of the day before, making light of her own part in it, but all the same she was gratified to hear the dismay in his voice—

"Karen! You could have been seriously hurt, even killed!"

She laughingly denied this, but Simon still grumbled at her daring, and it warmed her heart to have someone concerned for *her* safety. With a final enquiry about his mother, she rang off, and then stood beside the phone, her lovely face pensive, her wide generous mouth soft at her thoughts.

It would be so easy to lose her heart to Simon, wouldn't it? Their worlds were far apart, and yet they were fast becoming close friends. He was an attractive man and she couldn't help knowing that he admired her, or perhaps it was because she was sorry for him and could see a side of the picture that others couldn't? With a sigh she turned away to see Penny coming through the door.

"Just a moment, Penny . . ." She went to peep in at Ricky—he was fast asleep, and she closed the door gently, turning to the other girl.

"Hello, love, anything wrong? Did you want to see me?"

"Well, er—not really. Oh, yes I did . . ." Penny replied.

"M'mm, like that, is it?" laughed Karen. "What about coming through to my sitting-room, it's more comfortable. Got a few minutes to spare, have you?"

"Yes, I'm playing hookey." There was a faintly defiant look in Penny's eyes, and Karen wondered what was bothering her. Something certainly was, judging by the unhappy look on her usually smiling face! Two mugs of coffee later, she said—

"Okay, Penny, now suppose you tell me what's the matter?"

"Pete's the matter, that's what!" the young hostess exploded. "Oh, I know he has to make himself pleasant to all the guests, but he's getting far too friendly with that—that man-eating blonde!"

"Angela?" Karen frowned, worried by the outburst. "Oh, Penny, I'm sure you're wrong. She makes a play for everything in trousers—even the doctor. I'm sure Pete isn't interested in her—not like that!" Penny's slim finger was tracing the rim of her mug; the coffee in it growing cold, her winged brows drawn together in a worried frown.

"That's not all . . ." Karen waited for her to go on. "I'm sure I'm having a baby."

"Why, that's great news, love," and then seeing the look on the other's face, Karen finished, "it is, isn't it?"

With a shrug, Penny sighed deeply.

"I don't know. Here we are—in the middle of the season. I—we always wanted to have a family, but not yet. Oh, Karen, I don't know just how Pete will take the news right now. And if he's fancying

Angela . . ." Tears glistened in her troubled eyes. "I'm all mixed up, I don't know what to do."

Karen crossed the room and put a comforting arm around the unhappy girl's shoulders.

"As I see it, Penny love, there are two things you should do—and soon! One—tell Pete about the baby, and two—forget this utter foolishness about him and Angela. Now then . . ." and for the next few minutes her questions were purely clinical.

"I reckon you can finish this season, Penny, as long as you don't overdo things. Take a little rest when you can; ease off some of the more strenuous pursuits and so on. I'll keep a strict eye on you, my girl, as well as visits to the ante-natal clinic at the General Hospital here. And do cheer up—you want Pete's baby, don't you?"

"Well, yes, of course I do. But we did have so many good ideas, so many plans . . ." she murmured ruefully.

"And we all know what happens to plans, don't we, Penny?"

They both looked at each other and grinned, and Karen was pleased to see how

186

much brighter the other girl was looking when she left.

After she had gone, Karen stood at the little window, lost in thoughts and then, her mind made up, she left the Medical Unit to make her way over to the big house. As she was locking the door, she caught a glimpse of Joanne's bright yellow track suit.

"Hi, Joanne, how's things going? Enjoying your snorkelling?"

The young girl's face lit up.

"Oh yes, it's great! And—and Sandy's great . . ." she paused, her cheeks growing pinker, causing Karen to smile to herself knowingly.

"You like him, do you?" The other girl nodded. "And does he like you?" Karen went on gently.

"I think he does," Joanne paused, and then burst out, "but it's my father he's interested in really!"

Karen frowned, and then turned the key and opened the door again.

"Come inside, pet, we can't talk out here . . ."

Perched on the corner of the table, with

Joanne slumped in a chair opposite, she ordered—

"Now—tell me."

"Well, it appears that Sandy's always been keen on my Dad's books, and is dying to meet him. I reckon he just sort of puts up with me on the off-chance of meeting my father."

Poor child, she does have a rough time of it, Karen mused as she watched the other's downcast face.

"Sandy's got a degree in English—he wants to be a writer—he's dead keen on research, literature and that sort of thing, so of course, he'd like to get to know Dad and . . ."

"As I see it, Joanne, you ought to get them together—who knows, Sandy could well get to like you, too. And anyway, you wouldn't have your father disapproving of the friendship then, would you?"

Joanne's face brightened, and Karen rose and hugged her shoulder.

"Go on, pet, give it a try. And as I see it, you're a lovely change from all these glamorous pussies he has to fight off all the while . . ."

A few minutes later, Karen knocked on

the door of the Mannings' suite, and for once, Angela was in. She was blow-drying her hair, and frowned as she saw who it was . . .

7

"CAN I see you for a few minutes, Miss Manning?" Through the mirror, Karen saw the other girl's face shadow with impatience.

"What do you want now, nurse?"

"A favour really. And please—couldn't you call me Karen?—it sounds so much more friendly."

The blonde gave a nonchalant shrug.

"Why should I do you a favour?" she asked rudely.

"Let's say you owe me one for getting your mother off your back! Well—I wondered if you would like to help Penny —the hostess?"

Angela's pencilled eyebrows rose a mile in surprise, and Karen hurried on—

"She's having a baby. It's a secret yet, but I wondered if you could help her out with some of her duties?" She went on quickly before the other girl could flatly refuse. "You're so good at swimming and tennis and things like that. And so popular

190

with all the other young folks. I think you'd be marvellous. After all, you're here for ages yet, and it would certainly keep you from getting bored. And you would be doing Penny such a great favour," Karen stopped for breath and then plunged on, "I haven't mentioned this idea to anyone yet, of course. I thought I'd better see what you thought of the idea first. You're the ideal person . . ."

Karen hated the way she was laying on the flattery, but it was the only way she could think of to catch the other girl's interest.

"Please, Miss Manning—Angela, what do you say? Will you give it a try? Just help her out for a little while with the more strenuous things. She could trust you to work with Pete, whereas another girl might, well—get too fond of him! She knows you've got heaps of boyfriends of your own . . ."

There was a pensive look now on the other girl's face, and Karen found herself holding her breath, hoping Angela would swallow the bait.

"Well, I'd have to think about it; I wouldn't want to be tied down."

"Of course not. But everything is so free and easy here, isn't it? You would only have to give a hand where you could, when you could, and I know the other guests would take their lead from you."

Karen watched Angela's face intently as she spoke. The blonde girl was already picturing herself in the lead in all the entertainments, the others following. Oh yes, it had its possibilities and she would have the choice of all the best young men as they came and went. Yes, it would work out quite well, besides helping Penny. And for once, Angela saw herself in the rôle of Lady Bountiful!

"All right. I'll have a go at it, but no promises mind . . ."

"Oh thank you, Angela. I knew I was right in asking you. Thanks, I'll let Penny and Mr. John know, shall I? You are an angel . . ."

Later that day, she saw her employer and told him, with Penny's permission, all about it.

"I'm glad you fixed it all up, nurse. Thank you. Pete and Penny are under contract for the whole season, but I wouldn't like Penny to lose her baby."

He paused and smiled across at Karen.

"I reckon you're as much a social worker here, young lady, as a nurse. And I'm grateful." His voice was gruff, and Karen left his office feeling very pleased with her afternoon's work. Penny had called her a downright old conniver, and she grinned to herself.

Although she wasn't sure how things would work out with Angela, Karen had a feeling that, given half a chance, the blonde girl might just possibly live up to what was expected of her . . .

Whenever things were quiet, Karen tried to catch up with her letter writing. There were always letters from home to answer, and she had kept in touch as she had promised with her old room-mate, Sue, who seemed extremely interested to hear about Simon Asheby.

". . . are things getting serious between you two, Karen? Do let me know—he sounds rather dishy . . ."

Pensively, Karen sat nibbling the end of her pen. She was meeting Simon that afternoon, and she knew she had a decision to make . . .

The heat had become oppressive and sticky, with a feeling of thunder in the air; clouds rolled in darkly from the sea on their way inland, promising a squall or two of rain as they passed overhead. But Karen decided to risk the bad weather and set Brown Belle at a brisk canter up the hill towards the Asheby estate. But even before she reached the clump of trees which was their usual meeting place, she felt the spots of rain splash on her face.

Simon was already there and he reached up his arms to help her down and together they hurried for the shelter of the trees.

"Phew! There's going to be a storm." Karen took off her hard hat and shook it free of rain, glad to feel her hair loose again. "If there is—this won't be a good spot, will it, Simon?"

And she turned towards him . . . turned —into his waiting arms, and as they closed around her, her startled eyes widened, and his mouth came down with a sudden fierceness on hers.

For a glorious moment, she gave herself up to the thrill of his nearness, to the warmth of his firm lips. And then, remembering her resolution of the morning, with her palms spread wide on his heaving chest, she pushed him away. She could feel his heart pounding beneath her touch, and looking up into his eyes, she whispered—

"It's no use, is it, Simon? You and I, I mean? It's got to stop before we get in too deeply; before we both get hurt."

For a long moment, rebellious dissent showed in the shadowing of his dark eyes, and then he moved his head sorrowfully.

"You're right, Karen. It would be so easy to love you and forget all else. But I *must* marry where there is money— enough money to let me keep Asheby Manor—for my sons and their sons . . ."

He turned away suddenly so that she could not see his face.

"I suppose you'll hate me—a man who is willing to marry possibly without love —a man who would marry for money? But, my darling Karen, it is for a kind of love really—love of my inheritance . . ."

His voice was low and full of anguish, and Karen's heart ached for him.

"I know, Simon, and I *do* understand. And I don't hate you, and never will. You've always been honest with me, and

I—well, I had already decided this morning to tell you that we must not meet again, except by chance, in passing . . . It's not fair to either of us."

His face was wretchedly unhappy as he turned to her once more. Putting out a gentle hand, he traced the line of her jaw, touched the soft mouth, and a sound—almost a groan—broke from his lips.

"But, oh, Karen, it would have been so easy to love you," he repeated softly.

"And I you, but it's an impossible dream, Simon." Her throat hurt as the unshed tears pricked behind her eyelids. She looked up steadily into his face for a while, and then replaced her cap, saying softly—

"Look, the clouds are passing over. I must go now, Simon. I'll always have a special spot in my heart for you, and I hope, oh, how I hope—that you'll meet a nice girl soon. One that can help you keep your home. Let's say goodbye now, Simon, here . . ."

Gently, she reached up on tiptoe and pressed her lips to his, and then, putting her foot through the stirrup, she sprang up into the saddle, and without looking back, turned Brown Belle's head towards Coombe Magna—away from Simon and what might have been. And the tears blinded her eyes all the way back . . .

After she had handed the mare over to the stable boy, she walked slowly, heavy-heartedly, almost blind for once to what was going on around her. The sun had appeared once more and the guests were out in force again, determined to make the most of every moment.

The pool looked particularly enticing just then after the prickly heat. The turquoise tiles, the terracotta and white stucco of the patio; the colourful striped awnings, sunshades and deck-chairs, the sunbronzed holiday-makers reclining on the white-fringed chaises-longues—it was all so carefree, so happy, and so different from the sadness in Karen's heart right then.

Suddenly, there was a shout of dismay, a commotion at the shallow end of the pool. Children screamed, adults ran calling frantically. Swiftly Karen was on the alert, sensing danger as she, too, ran to the other end of the pool. To see, with shocked eyes, the body of a little girl and a tall young man gasping for breath beside her.

"Someone's drowned!" "A little girl—I saw her!" "I saw someone on the bottom —is she dead?"

Even as she ran, Karen heard snatches of the alarmed cries. The young man saw her and called out—

"Nurse! Nurse, thank God you're here . . ."

Without answering, Karen lifted the inert, sodden little body, and swiftly clearing a nearby table with one sweep of her arm, she laid the child down, the small head over the edge. Pinching the snub nose firmly, she applied her own mouth, clamping it tightly over the child's, and began to breathe deeply, rhythmically, mentally counting, breathing; her brain alert and clear; her mind praying that she would be in time.

It seemed ages before she finally felt a flutter, faint at first, and then growing stronger, as the child's lungs took up the rhythm and began to work of their own accord.

"Thank God . . ." How often as a nurse had she offered up her own silent prayer?

She turned the little girl over, gently laying her face sideways, firmly pressing, encouraging the water to seep from the bloated stomach. By the time the child was conscious, Karen's own clothes were soaking, mainly with perspiration, and she pushed back her damp hair, allowing the distracted mother to wrap her fast-reviving child close in a large towel and then a blanket.

"She'll do now—take her and put her to bed for a while. I'll change my clothes and come across to see how she's getting on. Please, don't worry, she's fine now," she repeated tiredly.

"How can we ever thank you, nurse?" The little girl's father, his face ashen and old-looking, wrung Karen's hand between his own, and then lifted his daughter tenderly.

Karen felt overwhelmingly tired as she went back hurriedly to her own quarters. But there was to be no respite for her, for before her hair was properly dried, she heard a knock on the surgery door.

"May I come in, Nurse Stevens?" It was Hannah Dobbs, the supervisor in charge of the children's crèche. "Never a dull moment, is there, with kids . . ." she began and then went on to tell Karen that she suspected an outbreak of German measles!

Karen sighed—and then remembered! German measles—had Penny been in contact with any of the suspect cases; was there any other newly-pregnant mother in the complex?

Putting on a clean white dress and cap, she followed Hannah to a couple of family bungalows, to see two miserable, flushed little children, to inspect their rashes and confirm Hannah Dobbs' suspicions.

"This'll spread like wildfire, I suspect, nurse?"

"Sure to. But it's the expectant mums who are at risk. This is nothing to worry about in itself; it's in early pregnancy that the trouble is caused," Karen answered worriedly.

Passing on instructions to the mothers; asking them to keep their children in quarantine for a few days, Karen hurried round to find Penny Naylor. But it was her husband, Pete, that she saw first, sports kit under his arm.

"Pete, I'm glad I found you—there's an outbreak of German measles," she began.

"That's all right, Karen, Penny's heard, and she told me that she was immunised some time ago."

"Thank goodness. See you, Pete."

As she passed the pool again, something made her pause, and she suddenly bent down and drifted her fingers through the water. It was freezing cold! No wonder there weren't many people in the pool right then. That was funny—the pool was newly-installed last year; the pump, generator and filter plant were neatly housed at one end beneath the wide ornamental steps which formed part of the sun terraces. Karen walked over to it, surprised not to hear any noise coming from it.

With a look of determination on her face, she approached a young gardener tidying the flower beds nearby.

"Will you get hold of old Mr. Rogers for me and ask him to come to the Medical Unit—at once, please!"

"I will that, nurse."

Karen checked that the little pool victim was recovering nicely, sitting up in her small bed and making much of the attention and fuss she was getting from her doting, grateful parents. But the memory of the limp little body made Karen's resolution stiffen when the old pool attendant came shuffling into the surgery a few minutes later.

"Sit down, Mr. Rogers," she indicated a chair and waited while he lowered himself stiffly into it.

"Why isn't the pool heated this afternoon?" As the old man started to prevaricate, she added firmly, "The pump isn't working either. I've checked for myself, and the test on the purity of the water I had made the other day showed that the filter isn't doing its job properly either. Well, Mr. Rogers. . . ?"

The old man's watery eyes met hers in silent appeal.

"That danged engine thing—I ain't no good with it. Showed me how to work it, them chaps did, but I ain't never got the hang of it. But the water's skimmed every morning—I'm good at clearing away the leaves an' things," he finished. And Karen remembered that he had formerly been a gardener on the Coombe Magna estate.

"Look, Mr. Rogers, a little girl was

almost drowned this afternoon. I'm not saying that the chilly pool caused it, but even in this hot weather, an outdoor pool should be heated a little. And certainly the filter plant must be working all the while."

She paused and then asked quietly—

"How old are you, Mr. Rogers?"

"I'll be 71 come September," he mumbled.

"Then don't you think you ought to retire, Mr. Rogers? Have a rest now, you've earned it. The pool, *and* the engine house, needs a younger man to understand how it works. Anyway, I'm sorry, but I'll have to report all this to Mr. John, you know. If I were you, I'd think about packing up the job, call it a day, m'mm?"

By the time the old man left, he had agreed to see Mr. John, and Karen made a note on her pad to do the same as soon as she got a chance.

From that moment on, things got busier than they had ever been since she came to Coombe Magna. To all appearances, the guests were a healthy, happy, fun-loving crowd, but all Karen and Hannah Dobbs and their little team of helpers saw were the poorly ones. One after another the children grew pink-eyed, sore-throated and feverish as spots appeared. Also one gangling teenager came in to see Karen, looking rather sorry for himself; his glands were slightly swollen and he had a rise in temperature. Karen spent an exasperatingly long time trying to discover from the boy's scatty-brained mother whether he'd had his polio jabs or not. Although Karen was sure the lad had glandular fever, she had to make sure and decided to get Matthew Henshaw to check him over.

"It's not catching, except perhaps through kissing . . ." she grinned at the disgruntled young man, who flushed crimson and shook his head. "Rotten luck on holiday; still I'll get doctor to give you something to make you feel a bit better."

Fortunately, it proved to be the only case, but she was landed with several German measles victims.

"Please, nurse, can I leave my two youngsters here . . . ?" came the frequent request during the next few days. Many young parents were loth to give up their precious holidays to stay indoors with sickly offspring. Not that they were heartless—more thoughtless, Karen reckoned.

All the same, she and Hannah Dobbs found themselves run ragged trying to keep fractious, itchy little boys and girls happily occupied.

John Lyle-Coombe came in to see how she was coping, and she had a chance to tell him about old Mr. Rogers.

"I'll find him a little job around the grounds, my dear. He'll never retire, and he's been with my family since he was a lad." The kindly boss's voice was almost apologetic, and Karen gave him a warm smile.

"That's all right, Mr. John, as long as the pool is looked after efficiently. Otherwise you'll be having the local MOH breathing down your neck . . ."

Angela Manning was thoroughly enjoying herself trying to outshine Penny as hostess-in-charge; still treating Pete as her special property, but apart from advising Penny not to let that worry her, Karen had to leave them to sort out their own particular problem. She was far too busy coping with the German measles outbreak; trying not to let it disturb the comfort of the older guests; endeavouring to let the parents enjoy their own holidays.

Her days and nights seemed to be spent between the Medical Unit and the kiddies' nursery quarters, and to her surprise she found Matthew Henshaw a tower of strength. He couldn't have been so busy just then at his own surgery, for half way through one morning Karen found him helping Hannah Dobbs in the crêche.

He was standing against a white-topped table, a large safety pin between his teeth, skilfully changing a baby's napkin!

"Don't look so surprised, Karen, I did my Maternity before I took my exams. No, you don't, young lady," he told the baby who was trying to eat the end of his tie. "Not good for the digestion; here, try this."

Looking quite at ease, he fed the baby its bottle, and his large hands were surprisingly gentle as he lifted the infant up to his shoulder, patting its back to fetch up the wind! And from the familiar way he and Hannah Dobbs talked to each other, she could see that he was no stranger to the crêche.

Between taking temperatures, Karen asked him—

"Lots of nephews and nieces in your family then, doctor?"

"Dozens! Eldest of a decent-sized flock, that's me. Anyway I love kids; you know where you are with them. Now take this young lady—you feed one end and keep the other dry and she's your friend—no questions asked!"

He tucked the contented baby back safely into her cot, and then joined the toddlers in the playpen, amusing them, comforting them, with a tenderness that delighted Karen. She was certainly discovering another side to this brusque young doctor, wasn't she? And it came to her then—was this why he was so keen on getting a new Maternity Centre? Penny had told her that the maternity wing of the old General Hospital was the "pits", and that she was wishing there was a better prem. baby unit—just in case . . .

But it was on that special night . . . A nurse shouldn't have favourites, but five-year-old Donna was such a sweetiepie that all the staff of the nursery, as well as Karen, secretly adored her. She had been left to play there "because the heat seems to be too much for her outside" her mother had told them. The child certainly looked flushed and her temperature was high. She complained that her head hurt, refused her food, and was dizzy when she moved around.

Rather worried, Karen took her across to the Medical Unit with her—it was quieter there and cooler, but when she tried to get Donna to drink some salted water, the child became so upset that it was difficult to get her to swallow it.

Donna's mother herself looked exhausted, apparently she had been up all the previous two nights trying to soothe the fractious child.

"I'll keep her here with me, Mrs. Wyndham. You go and try to get some rest; I'll take good care of her. I want to watch her temperature."

"You'll fetch me if—if she gets any worse, won't you, nurse?" Finally, Karen managed to persuade her to go across to her own bungalow to lie down. She had two other children to care for, too.

Karen returned to the little cubicle and switched on the cool air fan. It was still rather sticky and humid, and she wished the storm would break and cool the air.

Heat exhaustion was common in this type of weather, with everyone sweating and losing so much body moisture. She bathed little Donna's face in cool water; it was so hot and red and dry. Her fitful tossing was pitiful to watch; and Karen dreaded the long hours of the night.

She knew she must get Donna's temperature down before morning, and she repeatedly bathed the little body in cool water, but the child remained as hot and dry as ever; if only she could be induced to sweat again! Karen sat there beside the narrow bed with the quiet dark night outside; inside, the subdued light, the soft whirring of the fan, the fitful mutterings of young Donna. And Karen was once more transported back to the long night vigils she had known at St. Catherine's, but there she hadn't been alone. There had always been an experienced sister to call upon; there she had not been solely responsible, had she?

Suddenly, startling her out of her reverie, there was a soft tap on the door, footsteps she thought she recognised, and Matthew Henshaw's tousled head appeared from behind the curtain. He crossed quietly and stood looking down at the sick child, his fingers on her pulse.

"Heat stroke?" His voice was low and serious. Like Karen, he knew that the next few hours would be critical; the child's temperature must be reduced; the dry skin induced to start sweating again. "Want any help?"

"I can manage, but I'd be glad of your company for a while," she answered gratefully, acknowledging at last her need for this man.

Without being asked, he changed the bowl of water for some fresh and started gently to sponge down Donna's body. His hands, the tender concern in his eyes, brought a lump to Karen's throat, and she wondered how many other local GPs would do this after a day in the surgery and making house calls? When she tried to tell him what she felt, he shrugged off her thanks.

"I'm a sucker for kids," he said with a lopsided grin. "I hate to see anyone suffer, but when a child's ill, it twists me up inside somehow. You know, Karen, there was always someone down with something when I was at home, and I think I always wanted to be a doctor even as a very young lad. My parents had to sacrifice so much to keep me on at school, put me through medical college, and when Dad died it was even worse for my mother. The others were still too young to help themselves, and it seemed I'd got to give up my dreams of ever becoming a doctor. And then Professor Felstead started to help me. I can never thank him enough; he was like a second father to me."

There, in the quiet of the night, there could have been no one else in the world but the two of them and the sick Donna. They were close, as never before, with a close awareness that was a wonderful, tender thing. Matthew Henshaw's face was shadowed in the dim light and his voice was deep, full of feeling brought back by his memories.

"And so you'll marry the Professor's daughter . . ."

To Karen, sitting there, waiting, time was suspended; waiting for his reply— knowing and yet not knowing why, that it would be important to her.

"I'm not in love with Lisa Felstead,

Karen." She saw his eyes darken as they looked across into hers.

They renewed the water and started to sponge the small Donna once more, for she was still terribly hot and dry to the touch. If only the fever would break and the blessed sweating of the skin begin again? Karen's heart ached with anguish; Donna was such a pretty child even in her illness.

Seated across from each other, waiting, she asked—

"I suppose it's those early struggles of yours that makes you so keen . . ."

"To get my Maternity Centre?" he finished for her. "Yes, Karen, I want the very best treatment for all young mothers and babies, not just for the rich, but for the poor, too. The old maternity wards at the General Hospital are so out of date—we need special prem. units for the tiny babies. One day there'll be such an epidemic in those wards; the ante- and post-natal clinics are so crowded; there's no room for relaxation classes for the mums-to-be . . . nothing!"

As he spoke, Karen could feel the driving passion, the love of children, the force that made him what he was, and suddenly she was ashamed. Ashamed that she had thought him pig-headed, with a chip on his shoulder about the rich; especially the rich landowners, those who inherit great wealth without having to work hard for it. He didn't want money for himself—just for his cause—his dream for tomorrow.

"Why don't you go and try to get some rest, Karen? You look all in." Matthew's voice broke in on her thoughts. "Come on, my girl, up you get."

He reached across and half-lifted her to her feet, holding her firmly by the shoulders, and for one silly moment, she longed to put her head on that broad chest.

"I'm all right, I must stay . . ."

"Don't be daft, girl," his voice was gruff, "go and put your feet up. I'll call you if there's any change."

He leaned forward and placed his lips gently to her forehead and Karen's heart lifted. She was about to raise her lips to his—and then she drew back, not wanting to make more out of the little gesture than he possibly intended. Not wanting to take advantage of the situation, the closeness, the quiet of the night.

As she settled back on top of her bed, she felt a deep sense of comfort, of being secure and safe, with Matthew Henshaw on watch in the small cubicle next door.

"Karen—Karen, my dear . . ." Startled, she sat upright, her heart thudding rapidly until she realised where she was.

"It's going to be all right, Karen, she's sweating normally again! The temperature's down a little, too!"

Blinking against the tears of relief, Karen held out her hand and clutching the strong one nearest to her, she brought it up to her cheek, her lips, gratitude swamping her then.

"Oh, thank you, Matthew, I'm so glad," she whispered in a most unprofessional manner.

She hurried through to see that Matthew was right—the small girl was nowhere near so hot or red-looking; her tossing had quietened now as beads of sweat clung to the tiny upper lip, the smooth forehead. Karen turned a radiant face to Matthew's and as they smiled jubilantly at each other, both knew that something else, besides the recovery of Donna, had taken place there that night.

"You called me Matthew," the doctor said quietly, and she knew he was pleased.

And during the rest of the week, he was in and out of Coombe Magna at every possible moment; helping, advising, comforting and lifting Karen's heart with gratitude for his tenderness. At the end of that week, many of the guests went home to be replaced by others and taking their partly-recovered offspring with them, and Karen and Hannah Dobbs were both thankful for a breathing space. It always took the newcomers a day or two to settle in, to look around and take stock before rushing pell-mell into their holiday activities. And before the waiting-room at the Medical Unit began to fill once more.

"Try and take it easy, Karen, you're looking a bit tired." There was something in Matthew's voice that made her cheeks flush, and as she stood there looking at him, she made a pretty picture. Her soft skin was turning to an attractive apricot-coloured tan with one or two light freckles across the bridge of her tip-tilted nose.

Matthew Henshaw was a tall man, and the petite Karen, in her flat white nurses' shoes, barely came up to his chin. She remembered the shared confidences during the long night's vigil, and a pulse beat quickly in her slender throat. There was something electric in the air between them, but Karen was afraid. Afraid that if she made one tiny false move it could be destroyed—that fragile thing that was struggling to blossom between them. Afraid that Matthew Henshaw would once more be as he was when they had first met—sarcastic and brusque, making her feel ridiculous and always in the wrong . . .

Besides, what chance had she against Lisa Felstead and Angela Manning; he was still very friendly and charming to both those lovely girls, wasn't he?

Somehow she felt lonely, with no one of her own. Joanne was making headway with her Sandy; Penny, radiant in her early pregnancy had an adoring Pete, even Angela seemed a more contented person since she had so much to occupy her time.

And for once, Karen's nursing career didn't seem to be quite enough . . .

It was about five o'clock that Sunday teatime when she heard the phone ringing. Crossing her fingers and hoping there were no more epidemics, she picked up the receiver.

"Karen? Matthew Henshaw here. Pick up all the first-aid stuff you can muster and get over to the Bott's Lane crossroads . . ." his voice sounded breathless and anxious.

"What's happened, Matthew?"

"Damned awful smash. Get moving, love, we're needed."

Karen ran outside and commandeered the first car she saw, and with the help of its driver collected all the bandages, dressings and painkillers she could lay her hands on; flung into the car and begged the owner to take her to the crossroads.

Long afterwards, in her nightmares, Karen was to remember the sight that met her horrified eyes that late summer afternoon. A luxury coach, full of holiday-makers, had collided head-on with a huge juggernaut heavily laden with packing cases of steel machinery. Both vehicles were badly damaged; the front of the coach practically concertina'd like a pack of cards.

The injured were lying all over the road and grass verges, but many—too many— were still trapped amidst broken seats and crushed luggage within the wreckage.

"Karen—oh, good girl!" Matthew Henshaw, his face already streaked with dirt and blood, grabbed her arm. "Bring that stuff and follow me," he ordered the sick-faced driver who had given Karen the lift.

"See, Karen, in there—it's a young woman, trapped by her legs. They're trying to move whatever's pinning her down, but she's in great pain—and I can't reach her. Not enough room; I might fetch the lot down. Can you. . . ?"

"I'll try, Matthew. Give me the syringe."

There was only a few inches between the crushed debris, and once she had wriggled through the space, all she could see was the shoulder, arm and neck of someone badly trapped there. Jagged splinters, heavy steel, groaned and creaked around them. There was blood, lots of blood, and the hoarse, ugly moan of a human being in the depths of great pain.

"I'm coming, my dear. Can you hear me? Try and put your arm towards me if you can. I'm a nurse and I can help you. Can you hear me?" Karen repeated her request, louder this time.

There was still so much noise and heat and dust and the cries from the injured that she could hardly make herself heard. Then there was an answering croak, the sound of a struggle and gasps of pain, but blessedly a slim arm was released and came inching through to where Karen could just reach it. Reach it and give the relief of a shot of morphia.

"Lie still, lovie, they're going to get you out any minute now, lie still. I won't leave you." Quietly she soothed as the answering groans grew fainter as the drug took effect. The pulse seemed pretty strong, and Karen hoped the young heart would survive the shock.

Many of the injured lying on the grass verges needed emergency treatment, several had lost so much blood that she and Matthew had to set up drips on the spot. Ambulances were arriving to take away as many as they could ferry, but others needed urgent attention before they could be moved.

Karen's heart was heavy as she slaved away under Matthew's instructions, trying to give aid and succour to so many at the same time. Other medical help was arriving now, but there was so much to do . . . so much to do.

She had long since lost her cap; her hands and arms were scratched; her face dirty, her tights and dress torn badly where she had crawled in and out of the smashed coach; knelt on the roadside gravel. It was almost two hours before the last, the least injured, had finally been despatched to hospital.

"I'll have to get down there—they'll be needing every doctor they can get,' Matthew said, his face drawn and tired with the ordeal of the last two hours.

"Shall I come, too, Matthew?" Karen asked anxiously.

"No, my pet, you've done enough. Enough for two. You were great, Karen, no one could have done more. Get back to

Coombe Magna; you might be needed there anyway."

And he lifted her chin, dirt and all, and kissed her firmly on her trembling, soft mouth.

"Bless you, Karen . . ." and he was gone, leaving a bemused, exhausted but somehow happy Karen standing there watching his tall figure disappear.

Matthew Henshaw was not the only one to praise her. The Monday evening's local paper carried the full story with pictures. And Dr. Matthew Henshaw and Nurse Karen Stevens were greatly featured in that story; their coolness under stress; their unfailing skill and hard work, regardless of any danger to themselves was highlighted in glowing detail.

Oh yes, it was all there, with more than a hint of how lucky the local people were to have the services of such a devoted doctor in their midst! Karen read it all with shining eyes. At last Matthew's true worth was being appreciated. At last he was being accepted, no longer thought of as a "newcomer".

8

GOING about her job as busily as ever, Karen still had time to think over in her mind how she could possibly help Matthew to achieve his ambition. For, by then, she knew she wanted to help him fulfil his dream for tomorrow. If only she could persuade him to get rid of his prejudice against Simon and to some extent against John Lyle-Coombe.

It grieved her, too, to know that Matthew thought she was out to marry Simon for his wealth and position. Surely they were much closer now; he must know her better and realise that she wasn't the sort of person who would marry for those reasons?

As she went about her work, she chided herself for bothering what the doctor thought about her. But she did care, deeply, and she knew that his respect and regard were important to her peace of mind. She was annoyed with herself for letting the image of a rugged face, a pair of brown expressive eyes, a sensitive mouth haunt her days and nights. He was a pig-headed, stubborn north countryman—not her type really, and yet she remembered his gentleness with the little ones in the crèche, his tender concern over young Donna, and how his eyes had darkened as they looked into hers on the night of the road accident. She recalled, too, the sight of his tired dismayed face, the compassionate sag of his broad shoulders as they had toiled together at the scene of the crash.

He cared for the sick—really cared! To him, being a doctor was healing and caring —not something to do with money or making himself a fine career, as it was for someone like Keith Thomas . . .

Keith had been in her thoughts, too. In a recent letter from Sue she had been told that he had been enquiring about her—asking for her address . . .

". . . methinks our luscious Keith is chafing at the bit, Karen darling," Sue had written. "Rumour goes—and you must remember how rumours fly around here—that he's getting just a wee bit fed-up of being under his wife's thumb, to say nothing of her father's! *They* apparently don't treat him as a little tin god—more like a well-dressed errand boy! Serves him right, I say, for the callous way he treated you, Karen. You don't mention the dishy Hon. Simon lately; has he dropped out of your life, too? Tell me all your news in your next letter—I do miss our little gossip gatherings, love . . ."

Dear Sue, Karen missed her, too, although she had made many new friends at Coombe Magna. On her shopping jaunts into town lately, she had been greeted warmly by the shopkeepers, the teashop waitresses. And the local hospital was fast coming to regard her as a competent and trustworthy member of the nursing profession.

One fine morning, refusing young Ricky's offer of an escort, with Mrs. Roberts left in charge at Coombe Magna, Karen had been into town shopping for various staff colleagues who had to work, themselves, during shop hours. When she had finished her shopping, she strolled down by the tiny harbour. It was one of her favourite walks; she never tired of watching the weather-beaten-faced fishermen unloading their catch; watching the sun turn the harvest of the sea to silver, as the young men sluiced down the slippery decks. Watching the small boats bobbing at anchor; the small boys rowing frail-looking dinghies to and fro. The sights, the smells, the leisurely pace of the small harbour never failed to enchant her every time she found herself there.

Looking across to where the "Lillane" was moored, she saw a movement on deck. It was Simon, and suddenly she made up her mind to go and see him. One of the young boys was quite prepared to row her out to the boat for a small tip, and by the time they were alongside, Simon had seen her coming and was waiting with willing hands to help her aboard.

"Karen—what a lovely surprise . . ." he greeted her warmly.

"Hi, Simon. I've only got a few minutes. Could I talk to you, Simon? There's something I'd like to discuss with you, please."

With a quick glance at her face, he led her down below deck to the small compact cabin. It was immaculately clean; the woodwork beautifully polished, the brass-work gleaming, bunks stowed away neatly. Sitting her down comfortably facing him, he asked her—

"What is it about, Karen?"

She drew in a deep breath, nervous now the moment had come, and then she suddenly burst out—

"Simon—I'd like to tell just *one* person about what you confided in me. About why you needed to sell Asheby Bay; why you need the cash so badly."

He moved with a quick uneasy movement in his seat, and she hurried on—

"It's Dr. Henshaw, Simon, just him and only him, I promise. You see . . ." and she went on to explain to the listening man opposite her just why she needed to put things right with Matthew. "I'm sure I could make him understand, and what is more, he would respect my confidence. It would go no further. He's a stubborn man, Simon, as stiff-necked in his pride as you are in a way. Please let me tell him. You see, Simon . . ." her face flushed under the warm tan, "he thinks I'm after you for your money and title and Asheby." Her smile was twisted, wryly apologetic.

The man squared his shoulders, breathing in deeply. "It's important to you, is it, Karen, what the doctor thinks of you?" Simon's dark eyes were watching her face intently and she nodded. There was no need for lies or prevarication between her and this man.

"I'm afraid it does, Simon. And I'm fast coming to see that he's right about his new Maternity Centre. If only I could get him to go about the whole business in a different manner; to get rid of that whacking great chip on his shoulder, I think he might get more co-operation from the other doctors and the local people."

"Then, Karen my dear, if it means so much to you, you have my permission to explain to him—that I'm not really a money-grabbing, 'grind the serfs into the dust' type of landowner!"

Simon's smile was full of understanding, for Karen's face had given so much away, as usual.

"I wonder . . ." she began again, greatly emboldened by his warm smile, ". . . if Matthew and the others managed to raise enough money, would—would you sell them the land for the Maternity Centre?"

Her large hazel eyes were full of entreaty, beseeching him to say yes.

"With a little modification—yes, I think I might," Simon answered slowly, his eyes serious.

"If everybody got together—with enough money—and discussed it, properly and sensibly . . . oh, Simon," Karen's eyes were flecked with amber as her happiness flowed over. "Oh, bless you, Simon . . ."

She was so pleased with her morning's success, that she felt as if she could have walked on the water, without the need for the young lad's dinghy! She was so sure that she had really achieved something for Matthew!

To make the morning's happiness complete, the first person she saw when she ran up the harbour steps was Matthew, his fat old corgi in tow. He had been standing there watching the arrival of the small boat from the "Lillane".

"Matthew—just the person I want to see . . ." she exclaimed joyously, but his face was dark with anger and jealousy.

"What for, Karen? To tell me that you and Simon are to be married, is that it? Have you managed to hook yourself the Hon. Simon? Do you see yourself as Lady of the Manor?"

The bitterness in his harsh voice cut through Karen's happy daze like a sword, and she stopped, too astonished to go on, her eyes wide and tragic-looking.

"That is his boat, isn't it, Karen?" he snapped indicating the "Lillane" across the short stretch of water.

"But Matthew, you're all wrong, I've been to see Simon about . . ."

"Spare me the intimate details, please, Karen."

Karen didn't see the ragged pain in his brown eyes; she only heard the accusing, condemning words, and she put out a hand to detain him as he turned abruptly away, a rising sense of outrage at his absurd jealousy. He whistled his dog and Karen, suddenly aware of the interested onlookers around them, had to let him go. And she watched him with stricken eyes as he strode, stiff-backed, away from the harbour, leaving her there stunned and numb.

To make a bad morning worse, Karen had barely put down her parcels when the door to the surgery was thrown open and an irate Angela Manning stormed in, green eyes blazing.

"So much for trying to help people out," she said bitterly, "I shouldn't have let you persuade me to help that—that ungrateful Penny Naylor . . ."

Karen sighed; right then she didn't feel in the mood for further problems; she had enough of her own, but she managed to ask carefully—

"What's happened, Angela?"

"Penny has openly accused me of making a play for her husband! I can't help it if he finds me better company, more attractive, can I? Then she—she pushed me into the bathing pool—out there, in front of everyone, making them all laugh! Oh yes," she cried, her green eyes blazing with temper, "they all thought it very funny. Well, I didn't! And so, Nurse Stevens, I'm here to tell you that I'm quitting—leaving Coombe Magna at once! Mother and I have decided to go on a cruise until our place is finished. As for that Penny—her husband's welcome to do her job as well as his own. And a fat lot of thanks he'll get from her . . ."

It took Karen ages to talk the excitable girl into some sort of composure.

"Well, I hope you both enjoy the cruise, Angela. And I thank you for helping out with Penny's job. Please, don't be too upset. I'm sure she'll be sorry when she has time to get over her outburst. Put it down to her condition, Angela."

That young lady gave a loud sniff and shrugged disdainfully, and Karen hurried on—

"Shall I get one of the maids to help you pack? I'll let Mr. John know you're leaving, shall I? Please let me know if there's anything else I can do, won't you?"

Karen couldn't help thinking that Mrs. Manning was so much better for *her* stay at Coombe Magna, and once Angela had got over her temper, she would realise this, too.

Deep down in her heart, Karen was just a little pleased that the blonde girl was going away, for surely that meant that she and Matthew were not involved with each other. And Karen wondered if perhaps she had been a bit jealous of the effect of Angela's cool beauty on the doctor?

Outside, she found young Ricky and his shadow, Luke, both giggling hilariously.

"You should have seen her hair, nurse, and her face—all streaky it was." Obviously they had seen Angela's unladylike topple into the pool. "Bet it's the first time that bikini ever got wet!"

Trying hard not to smile with them, she shooed them off, as she saw the famous C. C. Thorpe approaching. Oh no, not more trouble, she moaned to herself.

"Good morning, nurse, I wonder if you can help me?" Mr. Thorpe's face wasn't exactly friendly, but it did seem a shade more relaxed than the last time she'd seen him. Perhaps the happy atmosphere of Coombe Magna was finally getting to him, she mused, as she ushered him into the surgery.

"What can I do for you, Mr. Thorpe?"

"Well, I've got an ear-ache." He pulled on his left ear, with a grimace. "Must have got some sand or something in it . . ."

Karen seated him on a stool, put a paper bib round his neck and carefully began to examine the offending ear with her otoscope.

"No sign of otitis—ear inflammation," she murmured, "but you do seem to have a build up of wax and so on, Mr. Thorpe."

"Can you do anything for it, nurse?"

Karen explained that she would apply some drops for a few days to soften the wax, and then give the ear a "wash-out" and so syringe away the blockage that was causing the trouble. She didn't like to tell him that this trouble often came with age, or to anyone in a particularly dusty job. As she worked, they talked about the pleasure Joanne's snorkelling lessons were giving her.

"Nice lad, that," he replied, much to Karen's surprise. She expected the writer to be annoyed at anyone taking his daughter away from him. "In fact, at the end of this season, I'm thinking of taking him on to help me. You know, with my research and so on; I'm working on a rather long saga and could do with his help."

Delighted; thinking how nice all this was for young Joanne, Karen cleared away her kit, asking Mr. Thorpe to come back in a couple of days.

The following week, there were more young people than ever arriving at Coombe Magna. The families taking advantage of the quieter, less expensive part of the season had been and gone, so had most of the older people. Now it was the turn of the younger couples; the business types, freed for a while from their office desks.

Penny was looking particularly radiant now that the first queasy weeks of her pregnancy were over, and with her husband's help she looked as if she would be able to cope with her job quite well. The younger crowd were much more to her liking, and she was determined to enjoy this—probably her last—season before being tied down with a new baby!

Jake Brownlow was one of the liveliest new arrivals, although he came with his right ankle in plaster, having sustained a Pott's fracture through getting it twisted in a rabbit-hole whilst playing a round of golf the week before his holiday was due! But this didn't stop his being the life and soul of the party at whatever activity was going on! There he was in the thick of things, using his crutch as if he'd been used to it all his life. His plaster cast was soon adorned with the scrawled signatures of the rest of the crowd, and altogether he was a thoroughly nice, likable chap.

Karen wasn't a bit surprised though when he was brought into the Medical Unit one morning as she was clearing up after a full session of minor injuries. His face was rather grey-looking and he was obviously in pain, and there was a wide crack in the plaster round his damaged right ankle!

"You'll have to go down to the General Hospital with this, Jake, my lad. I'll borrow Mrs. Roberts' car and run you there if you hang on for a few minutes. Keep still . . ." she warned.

Leaving Mrs. Roberts in charge, she took Jake to have the damage investigated and the plaster renewed, and then decided to call in at the doctors' for some prescriptions she wanted.

"I'm in no hurry, nurse. Miss Felstead here'll keep me company, won't you, Miss Felstead?" Jake's impudent, boyish grin won an answering smile from the secretary, much to Karen's surprise. The dark-haired girl flushed and hurried round to place a chair handy as Jake manoeuvred his crutch with ease.

Matthew Henshaw frowned at the interruption as he looked up from the papers he was working on before him. A shadow passed over his face as he saw who his visitor was . . .

"Matthew—I must see you. Lisa tells me you are free for a little while." She sat down, determined not to be put off, although her heart was beating rapidly against her ribs, making her voice husky as she went on—

"I just wanted to tell you that I'm not going to marry Simon Asheby, and never ever thought of doing so. Neither did he. I'm not in love with him, and he has to marry someone with money enough to help him keep going at Asheby Manor . . ."

Watching the changing expressions come and go across the rugged face before her, she told him, clearly and without rancour, all that she knew of Simon's circumstances.

"He has promised me that—if enough money can be raised to give him a fairly decent price for it—he *will* sell you the piece of land you want, Matthew. I suggested that maybe if you all got together and sorted the matter out again —well, it could just work out. With the government grants and everything . . ."

"So you've succeeded where I failed, Karen?" Matthew mused bitterly. "He'll do for you what he wouldn't do for me, eh? And yet you tell me he's not in love with you?"

Karen felt her anger rise, and her brown eyes flashed,

"I told you—there's nothing between us. There can't be—and won't be. Why do you keep on saying. . . ?" she broke off, her voice thick with threatening tears of frustration.

"I'm sorry, Karen, I can't help being jealous. He has so much to offer you. More—much more—than a lifetime of hard work and struggle—against sickness, blind prejudice and near-poverty."

Karen rose to her feet blindly.

"I must get back, Matthew. Anyway, you know how . . ." and, her eyes full of tears, she stumbled out of the room and into Lisa Felstead's little cubicle.

There she found the girl laughing and joking with Jake like old friends; she could scarcely believe the change she saw in Lisa's face; she would never have thought she could look so different! Her cheeks were flushed a rosy pink, her blue eyes full of laughter, and she seemed to be hanging on every word the smiling Jake uttered!

"Ah—ready to go, nurse? I'll be seeing you then, Lisa. I'll give you a ring, may I?"

"Yes, please, Jake. 'Bye."

If Karen hadn't felt so sick at heart, she would have gaped in astonishment at the change in Matthew's secretary. But she wasn't to know that the doctor had recently made it quite plain to Lisa that he would never think of her as other than a very dear friend, and that the girl had decided at last that she had better try to forget her feelings for him—and begin to look elsewhere—to make a life for herself away from the doctor's.

Lisa had been attracted almost immediately by the spontaneous gaiety of Jake Brownlow; it was a case of the attraction of opposites. Her serious, lovely face had appealed to him at once and he wanted to see more of her, to make her smile, and their attraction was to grow at every meeting.

Meanwhile, Karen grew restless and curiously dispirited in spite of the loveliness of the golden summer and the beauty of her surroundings. She dragged through each day, still as efficient on the outside as ever, as calm as ever, but, inside, her heart was heavy with a puzzling ache, a sense of loss . . .

"Is the heat getting you down, love?" Mrs. Roberts asked, her homely face full of concern.

Karen certainly looked peaky as if she hadn't been sleeping well; she had lost weight, too. Probably dieting, silly girl! Still that didn't account for the absence of her usual ready smile, did it?

"Too many late nights, Karen?" she pondered.

"No, Mrs. Roberts, it's just that . . ." Karen began and then paused. Just what? She shrugged aimlessly. "I'll take a dip in the pool; it'll freshen me up. Will you be all right here?"

But before the other woman could

answer, the telephone rang and Karen went to answer it.

"Karen? Is that you, darling?" For a couple of seconds, Karen could not remember the voice, and then it hit her! It was Keith. Only he would have the nerve to call her darling after what had happened.

"Oh, hello, Keith. Nice to hear your voice. How are you?" She was pleased to note how impersonal her voice sounded.

"Not too bad, Karen. Look, I'm on my way up to a medical conference; can I pop in and see you?" His voice, as imperious as ever, sounded as if he was in the next room, and not miles away in London.

"I—l don't know, Keith. I'm always pretty busy," Karen replied.

"Not all the time, surely, darling? Anyway, I'll be along about noon tomorrow. Try to make a little time for me; I do so want to see you again, Karen."

The old charm, the persuasive, captivating manner was still there, and Karen was pleased to see what little effect it had on her. Before she could demur, he called—

"Must ring off, sweetie, be seeing you. 'Bye," and the phone went dead.

Vanity made her change into a crisp, clean white dress and cap the next lunch-time, but then she scolded herself for bothering when, by twelve-thirty, Keith had still not put in an appearance. She had told Mr. John that she was expecting a friend from her St. Catherine's days to call.

"Give him lunch in the main dining-room, nurse. My own table will be free—use that," he told her generously.

It was nearly one-thirty before Karen saw the huge, opulent-looking saloon car drive into the rear entrance to stop outside the Medical Unit, directed there, as it turned out, by the Reception office.

She watched the once so-familiar figure of Keith Thomas climb from the wheel, still as fair and good-looking as ever, but she noticed how he had changed in several little ways. He had the beginning of a "bay window" stomach, she thought with amusement, and his mouth had a petulant, discontented droop to the corners that surely hadn't been there before?

Had she really once thought herself to

be madly in love with this rather pompous-looking young man? She went out to meet him, to be greeted effusively, loudly— "Karen, my love, you're looking lovelier than ever," and to her consternation, he kissed her soundly. "This sea air certainly agrees with you, and what a smashing tan you've acquired, darling."

The regular use of the word "darling" was still there—so rarely used up here in the north, so that now it sounded artificial.

"Hello, Keith," she replied coolly. "You're looking very well yourself."

His suit must have cost a small fortune and his shirt, cravat and shoes were all exclusively custom-made. Nice to have a rich wife, she thought to herself, whilst saying aloud,

"Let's get over to the dining-room, shall we? It's getting late for lunch."

"I know, sweetie. Sorry, but there was a devilish amount of traffic on the motorway coming up."

In the dining-room, his appearance caused a mild stir, and Karen knew there would be a lot of questions to answer afterwards. Almost at once, Keith launched into a long tale of woe. His wife definitely didn't understand him—he was sick and tired of not "being his own man"—of being at his father-in-law's beck and call!

Reading between the lines, as it were, Karen could see that Keith was badly missing the adoration he had received at St. Catherine's. As the meal progressed, he grew more and more sentimental; one would almost have thought he was carrying a torch for his former sweetheart, and would only need the slightest encouragement to take up that flame where it had been dimmed by his marriage!

Karen found her anger rising more and more as course followed course. What a nerve he had! Did he really think she would be willing to be his "little bit on the side" for old times' sake? Up here, where no one knew him; he would be quite safe, and oh, how he needed someone to bolster his wilting ego! The meal dragged on until the waitress began clearing away around them.

"Let me show you around the grounds, Keith, before you go. I'm free until evening surgery . . ."

"They work you long hours here then,

Karen, my dear?" he was ready to commiserate.

"Not really, but I do have regular off-duty times just the same as at St. Catherine's," she answered shortly.

"Ah, St. Catherine's—those were the days, eh sweetie?" he sighed extravagantly as if those days were eons ago. Karen restrained her smile.

As they strolled round the lovely grounds, Karen found herself getting more and more bored with Keith's inane chatter; mostly about himself and his wife's shortcomings; amused by his constant assumption that Karen was ready to fall, like a ripe plum, into his arms again!

She gave him a cup of tea about four o'clock, and when he began to press for another meeting, she told him firmly—

"It's no use, Keith, it's all over between us. You killed stone dead any affection I once had for you. And if you persist, you will destroy any regard I still have left for you. Please—go back to your wife. It's been nice seeing you again, but don't come again. I'm sorry . . ."

Keith's face was a study; he couldn't

believe his ears! He so obviously thought Karen would welcome him back with open arms. His ego had received a shattering blow. Nevertheless, as he said goodbye, he reached forward and planted a long kiss on Karen's reluctant mouth before getting into his car and roaring away. As she turned back to the surgery with a gesture of near disgust, she bumped into the figure of a man standing there, a witness to that affectionate little scene . . . Matthew!

Oh no! Of all the rotten luck—that he, of all people—should see and no doubt misunderstand Keith's effusive farewell! Her heart sank with the force of a stone, and for once she was speechless. If only Matthew hadn't seen that kiss . . .

And then as dismay swamped her, there came the revelation—she was in love with Matthew Henshaw! And it was as if there were suddenly a thousand candles where there had been only one. The ache of the last few weeks was explained, and for a few breathless moments, she wanted to go and hide. To hug the knowledge, the wonder, to herself.

She loved Matthew Henshaw—that obstinate, tender, pig-headed, wonderful man—who thought she couldn't possibly want a life of hard work. Suddenly she knew that all she ever wanted was to be with him; at his side wherever he was, to share his life, for always and ever. And her whole body was suffused with a radiance she had never known before . . .

So great was the surge of love that overwhelmed her then, she thought he must be aware of it too, but the doctor was too filled with the black jealousy raging in his own heart.

"Another conquest, Karen?" he said sarcastically, his hurt a jagged edge round the bitter words. "Another rich conquest by the look of that car . . ." he jibed. Pain darkened his brown eyes, and in spite of his anger, Karen rejoiced. He was jealous —he was jealous!

With true feminine illogic, she wanted to treasure the knowledge, to make him suffer a little longer. Then the urge to be in his arms became too strong and she said shortly—

"An old acquaintance from St. Catherine's, Matthew, that's all. On his way to a medical conference—a rather silly, flirtatious type . . ." and her contemptuous dismissal of Keith told its own tale.

"You're early for surgery, aren't you?" she asked.

Karen saw a shadow of sadness pass over his rugged face.

"I've been walking. I found my old corgi dead—in his basket—this afternoon."

"Oh, darling. Matthew . . ." she flew into his arms; his hurt was her hurt, and she wanted to comfort him as she would a small boy. She put up her arms, pulling his head down to hers, and their lips met in a wonderful first kiss; a tender kiss that grew with passion into something fierce and heart-clutchingly real. He held her at arms' length after a while, murmuring—

"I've wanted to do that since the very first time I saw you, darling. You can't possibly be in love with me . . . can you?" And the longing in his voice lifted her heart as if it had wings.

"You and no one else," she told him and the next few minutes were theirs and theirs alone.

"I'm so sorry about your dog, darling."

"He was getting old and it was a

peaceful end, but I shall miss him. Perhaps I shouldn't have brought him up here; he didn't take very well to being transplanted, Karen." He paused and looked down at her closely. "People don't either, do they?"

And Karen knew the words held a question.

"Look, Matthew—would your dog rather have stayed at home without you, or come up here with you, whom he loved? Well, it's the same with people, especially women in love."

She reached up and kissed him tenderly.

"As long as I'm with you, Matthew, just anywhere will do . . ."

"And I've been as miserable as hell thinking you wanted Simon Asheby," he smiled at her, confident now in her love.

"And I thought you wanted Lisa Felstead," she retaliated.

It was a radiant-looking Karen who went about her duties after that, her feet hardly seemed to touch the ground, and for once things at Coombe Magna seemed to be going smoothly all round. Old Mr. Rogers was now happily pottering round his precious flower beds, whilst a younger man had taken over the care, maintenance and supervision of the bathing pool.

John Lyle-Coombe had released Penny from her contract, and as soon as they could be suitably replaced, she and Pete were leaving; he to take a job in a hotel, she to await her baby's arrival. In the meantime, an equally radiantly happy Joanne was helping out in the organisation of the games and so on . . .

Angela Manning and her mother had departed for their cruise—and both were strangely missed. "It takes all sorts . . ." Karen mused when she realised this, but Mrs. Manning had announced firmly that they would be back, and she gave Karen a pretty little beaded evening bag as a parting gift. And watching the easy way in which she clambered into the waiting taxi, the nurse could not help but be pleased at the improvement in *that* patient, at least!

Perhaps she should have touched wood; it certainly didn't pay to get too complacent when you're nursing, did it? It happened so suddenly, too . . .

Practically all of the resort's guests had been watching a display of dancing by a local group of folk dancers, and then joining in afterwards with more enthusiasm than skill! Amongst these was Mr. John, pleased to see his guests enjoying themselves so much; doing a duty dance before sneaking away for a quiet game of billiards with his own cronies.

A few minutes later, one of the waiters rushed up to Karen as she sat recovering her breath after a brisk polka.

"Nurse—come quick, it's the boss . . ."

One look at the man's shocked face, and Karen ran with him to the billiards room. There she found Mr. John collapsed and obviously in great pain. His usually florid-looking face was pale and he was struggling to get his breath.

"Open all the windows," she called. "Here, help me get him on to the table." Willing hands lifted the suffering man on to the wide green expanse of the billiards table as Karen loosened his collar and tie.

She couldn't feel a pulse beat, and she grabbed a large cushion to put under his legs, and then with a hard, determined blow, struck the broad breastbone sharply. For what seemed an age, Karen leaned over, two hands flat, one over the other

—jerking hard in regular motion. Up and down, up and down, with the perspiration dripping from her brow. She kept it up until at last she could feel his heart flutter feebly and then take up its own beat once more,

The pulse rate was poor, but at least she could feel it again, and she straightened her back painfully, almost on a sob of relief. God—that was a near go . . . !

She made him more comfortable, and then turning to the waiter, asked him to get rid of the ring of curious faces staring down with anxious eyes.

"Please—he needs all the air he can get. Thank you. Watch him, I won't be a second . . ." and she ran as fast as her feet could carry her to the Medical Unit. Mr. John needed a shot of morphia to ease the pain of the coronary thrombosis. Whilst there, she rang the hospital, reporting in a few crisp words what had happened, and indeed, she had barely given John the injection before the ambulance men were here with the stretcher to take him to hospital.

It was a long night, and as Karen paced the small waiting-room, she understood once more just what the worried relatives of such emergencies had to endure. At last, the young doctor on night duty came in to tell her—

"He'll do, nurse, thanks to you," and he went on to give her all the clinical details. "You can see him for a couple o. minutes." And he had no need to tell her that she must not disturb the patient.

John's face was a better colour then, and the monitor bleep-bleeping away at his bedside showed that his heartbeat was improving, too.

She had a long, lonely walk back to Coombe Magna, giving her time to think to collect her thoughts. She was quite fond of her bluff, genial boss, and the sudden heart attack had upset her very much indeed. The assistant manager was waiting for her when she got back.

"We'll manage fine, Karen, until he's fi again. He will get over this, won't he?"

"This time, yes. But he'll have to ease up a lot, you know. Cut down on a few things in his diet, unload the stress of this place, take it easier a bit all round—that sort of thing. Yes, I'd say he'll be out o hospital in a week or two. Till then, we'l all have to do our best to manage without him, h'mm?"

"Don't worry, we will, Karen. Now you get off to bed, you look pooped, love."

The next day when she went to the hospital, John was sitting up in bed and looking much better.

"Hello, nurse. They tell me that you saved my life," he began bluntly.

"Well, let's say that it was lucky I was on the spot. Speed's the thing in cases like yours, Mr. John."

"I've been thinking, my dear. Time to think things over in here. The young doctor here tells me that the town could really do with a special little heart unit; small ambulance with a resuscitator and everything laid on—sort of flying squad for heart attacks."

"Most towns have one—even more," Karen replied evenly. John's face looked pensive, and she added quickly, "Don't worry about anything right now," but he lifted a thick hand and motioned her to be quiet.

"I've been thinking, too, nurse—that young doctor Henshaw of yours is right! We *do* need a new Maternity Centre, with better equipment, special units, for young mothers like our Penny, don't we? And I'm going to see that we get it . . ."

Karen's eyes shone with delight, and she squeezed the hand lying on the snowy white bedcover.

"Simon Asheby's promised the land if funds can be raised."

"We'll see, lassie, we'll see," and with that she was content.

"Now you just lie there and take a good rest. Things are going fine at Coombe Magna, Mr. John. You've got a grand lot of staff and they're coping just fine," she repeated.

She just had to see Matthew—to tell him all the news, so she hurried across to his surgery. For once, Lisa Felstead greeted her almost cordially; her romance with Jake Brownlow was certainly making *her* a lot happier-looking, Karen thought with amusement.

Matthew's face lit up when she went in to see him; his thick hair was as tousled as ever, his rugged face crinkled into the lopsided grin she loved so much, and her heart sang like a bird to think this lovely man was hers . . . hers. She hugged him close, returning his kiss with such fervour, that he held her at arms' length, looking down into her flushed face with delight.

With a rush, she began telling him all her employer had said.

"You'll get your new Maternity Centre now, Matthew. I just know you will, darling . . ."

Her bubbling enthusiasm was infectious, and Matthew grinned down into her excited face.

"And you, Karen—will I get you? Are you going to stay up here with me—amongst these stubborn northerners?—a couple of southerners in a strange land! To be my wife, my blessed helpmate? I do love you, little Karen, and there's so much we could do, you and I, together . . ."

Karen snuggled closer in his arms.

"That sounds great, Matthew—you and I together . . . with a dream for tomorrow . . ."

GUIDE
TO THE COLOUR CODING
OF
ULVERSCROFT BOOKS

Many of our readers have written to us expressing their appreciation for the way in which our colour coding has assisted them in selecting the Ulverscroft books of their choice.

To remind everyone of our colour coding—
this is as follows:

BLACK COVERS
Mysteries

★

BLUE COVERS
Romances

★

RED COVERS
Adventure Suspense and General Fiction

★

ORANGE COVERS
Westerns

★

GREEN COVERS
Non-Fiction

ROMANCE TITLES
in the
Ulverscroft Large Print Series

THE SHADOWS
OF THE CROWN TITLES
in the
Ulverscroft Large Print Series

The Trial of Charles I	*C. V. Wedgwood*
Royal Flush	*Margaret Irwin*
The Sceptre and the Rose	*Doris Leslie*
Mary II: Queen of England	*Hester Chapman*
That Enchantress	*Doris Leslie*
The Princess of Celle	*Jean Plaidy*
Caroline the Queen	*Jean Plaidy*
The Third George	*Jean Plaidy*
The Great Corinthian	*Doris Leslie*
Victoria in the Wings	*Jean Plaidy*
The Captive of Kensington Palace	*Jean Plaidy*
The Queen and Lord 'M'	*Jean Plaidy*
The Queen's Husband	*Jean Plaidy*
The Widow of Windsor	*Jean Plaidy*
Bertie and Alix	*Graham and Heather Fisher*
The Duke of Windsor	*Ursula Bloom*

FICTION TITLES
in the
Ulverscroft Large Print Series

Enquiry	*Dick Francis*
Flying Finish	*Dick Francis*
Forfeit	*Dick Francis*
High Stakes	*Dick Francis*
In The Frame	*Dick Francis*
Knock Down	*Dick Francis*
Risk	*Dick Francis*
Band of Brothers	*Ernest K. Gann*
Twilight For The Gods	*Ernest K. Gann*
Army of Shadows	*John Harris*
The Claws of Mercy	*John Harris*
Getaway	*John Harris*
Winter Quarry	*Paul Henissart*
East of Desolation	*Jack Higgins*
In the Hour Before Midnight	*Jack Higgins*
Night Judgement at Sinos	*Jack Higgins*
Wrath of the Lion	*Jack Higgins*
Air Bridge	*Hammond Innes*
A Cleft of Stars	*Geoffrey Jenkins*
A Grue of Ice	*Geoffrey Jenkins*
Beloved Exiles	*Agnes Newton Keith*
Passport to Peril	*James Leasor*
Goodbye California	*Alistair MacLean*
South By Java Head	*Alistair MacLean*
All Other Perils	*Robert MacLeod*
Dragonship	*Robert MacLeod*
A Killing in Malta·	*Robert MacLeod*
A Property in Cyprus	*Robert MacLeod*

MYSTERY TITLES
in the
Ulverscroft Large Print Series